GLORIOUS
NEMESIS

GLORIOUS NEMESIS

LADISLAV KLÍMA

Translated from the Czech by Marek Tomin

TWISTED SPOON PRESS

Prague

This translation was made possible by a grant
from the Ministry of Culture of the Czech Republic.

GLORIOUS
NEMESIS

1

When Sider travelled through the Alpine town of Cortona for the first time, the majestic landscape made such a strong and peculiar impression on him that he got off the train at the next stop and went back. The three days he then spent there were the most enchanting of his entire life. A poetic, golden shimmer such as he had never known before constantly suffused his soul; ever more mysterious, monumental sensations surged from his soul against his will, and though indistinct, it was just this lack of clarity that made them so immensely exhilarating. He often felt that these presentiments were about to reveal their essence — but at that very moment they always took flight with lightning speed to unattainable distances. The entire world intoxicated him, existence itself was his lover, songs erupted from his inner being, and at night he was embraced by magical dreams . . . Yet there was something darkly and powerfully horrifying about it all; in the deepest depths he was certain the most terrible abyss gaped beneath all this radiance.

Was all this being drawn out of him by the exterior surroundings? He was unable to come up with an answer. Although the views of the vast, glacier-lit mountains on all sides, the footpaths snaking over them, and of the town's diverse houses sparked within him miraculous flashes of monstrous sentiments, he always had to ask : Is this not after all my inner being overflowing with light that is casting its rays onto these objects so that their reflections, as if alien gifts, might be reabsorbed into the maternal All-Womb? This entire exterior world seemed so mystically familiar to him — yet again he had to ask himself : Do the depths of the soul not know everything, everything? Is there anything that has for all eternity not been the property of the soul? How else could it even see and hear? Isn't all seeing merely the flight back to the soul of all the mysterious birds that have ever left the eternal nest?

He left that bewitching place only because circumstance forced him to . . . , and as soon as it had disappeared from his eyes, so did the mysterious shimmer at once vanish from his soul, giving way to a singular despondency and revulsion. But even now he had to pose himself the question : Isn't it just coincidence that at this very moment I am experiencing an inevitable mental drain? Perhaps some form of deep autosuggestion is also at work, though there's nothing supernatural, nothing miraculous about what has so enticed me. —

He made a firm resolution to take up permanent residence in Cortona as soon as the possibility arose. —

After a year dominated by dull yet delightful recollections of those three days, he was able to make good on his decision. —

It was May, and Sider was twenty-eight years old. He had a delicate, enigmatic, handsome, manly face, beneath whose strength writhed something fractured, profoundly ominous, which to a perceptive soul spoke of predestination to a terrible fate. He was well off and entirely independent. —

2

When he arrived in Cortona, jaded by the long journey but also excited by expectation, the sky was gloomy, the mountains almost invisible.

Later he would blame these circumstances for the fact that there was no hint his mood from the previous year might return, and during the days that followed, his frame of mind was such that it was impossible to imagine anything worse. Disappointment, the greyest disgust. Such often happens when something is anticipated with inflated expectations; but Sider felt that the extent of his disillusionment was in no way proportional to his hopes, even though they had been considerable . . .

The whole of May was abominable : clouds, rain, snow, windstorms, mud, cold, virtually unabated. And when the sun did come out, it was as if it were only for its light to enhance the ugliness of the countryside. How dead everything was, how spiritless the mountains! They grimaced just like the lifeless mementos of a dead life, like reproaches for something irretrievably lost : Sider felt a growing nausea, a kind of fear crept into his soul and seemed to be rapidly setting down permanent roots.

Two things in particular continued to infuse him with mystical dread. Stag's Head, a mountain looming directly over the town — 2500 metres above it, 3500 metres above sea level — from whose broad crown protruded several thin, cone-shaped rock massifs like small horns. And an ancient, almost black two-floor cottage at the end of a lane that ran into a narrow ravine, a steep cliff poised directly above it — —

Otherwise, his life flowed by, tediously. He met with no one, he understood very little of the local language. The place was still deserted, the summer visitors yet to arrive, but one thing still managed to vividly colour the greyness of his days.

His fantasies had always nurtured the striking image of a woman. Indistinct, flickering, and yet powerful, promising him a peculiar lucidity of mind and warming his soul with furtive delights. Often appearing in his dreams, the images of Her were contradictory, though after waking he would never doubt it had been — Her. And now he had dreamt that he'd suddenly glimpsed Her high up on Stag's Head, a dream so lucid that even after waking in the morning he momentarily had the impression She was standing before him, so intense the phantasm and the onrush of mystical forebodings that his soul shuddered in its innermost depths. But in the blink of an eye he was no longer able to conjure up the vision again in his soul.

The first day of June was rainier than any before. Sider decided to leave Cortona forever on the following day. In the early evening, having made everything ready for his departure, he went out for a walk in the forest that lined the foot of Stag's Head just beyond the small town.

Half an hour later he was on his way back in a foul mood, his clothes and boots soaked through. The sky, however, was finally beginning to turn blue. The mountains to the east were illuminated by a yellow setting sun. He was walking through a rocky ravine, sparsely covered with trees and bushes. The place was wild and romantic and created the illusion of being far, far away from the places inhabited by people, though paradoxically he could hear dogs barking, cocks crowing, and children shouting.

He was coming to a bend in the path when — suddenly — two women emerged, approaching him. Absorbed in thought, he didn't raise his head until they were three paces away. He first looked at the woman farthest from him — dressed in red — and his body gave a jolt.

She was about twenty-five, beautiful, pale, and had an interesting face that harboured a noticeable restlessness — from a distance she reminded him of his vision. Though overall she was not very similar to Her, she still mysteriously evoked his dream image so powerfully that he unwittingly came to a halt.

That's when his eyes fell upon the other woman, wearing a cerulean blue dress, just as his elbow nearly brushed hers on the narrow path. And . . . — at once he staggered, his eyes went dim, he felt as if a hammer had struck his head. Only his embarrassment before the women prevented him from collapsing. It seemed to him that the woman in red made a movement to support him; he frowned and hurried on unsteadily. He did not turn round, but felt certain that they had stopped and were standing there observing him.

He finally recovered his wits only when he reached the garden of a restaurant. "After them!" was the thought that came to him. He looked round; he could not see them. He remained standing there for some time, uncertain of what to do. Then he took a seat in the garden and waited late into the night, hoping they would come back that way. They did not.

In all his life his soul had never felt so strange, so blissful, so horrified. The woman in blue was entirely, entirely the epitome of his dream vision, as if his phantasm had metamorphosed into a hallucination — —

•

He gave no thought to leaving. Moreover, the sky had cleared up for good and the beauty of spring finally erupted with full force. Sider's soul also brightened — and was revisited by some of the previous year's enchanting radiance. Once again, the terrible mountains and hospitable forests spoke to his soul in their mysterious dark tongue. For Sider was now — in love . . . — But what was the strange dread that, like a bass line, underscored the song in his soul? . . . Yet nothing in music save the sombre beating of a drum has such a monumental effect as the powerful black tones of a bass, nothing in the world is more beautiful than horror.

He spent his entire days crisscrossing the town and its surroundings, searching for his women. He did not find them. Nor was he able to discover anything about them. A week had passed since that wet, yellow-hued dusk, and Sider said to himself painfully : They were obviously foreigners, only passing through Cortona, — I'll never set eyes on them again!

As if everything a human sees, everything desired, everything thought must not necessarily become manifest and visualized and realized over and over, as if the force animating all things were not desire and yearning and Will . . .

•

It was a beautiful Sunday afternoon, 8 June. Sider was sitting in the garden of the restaurant that backed onto the forest. A band was playing to entertain the numerous guests — many summer visitors had gathered during the week. The music had lulled Sider into a deep dreaming . . .

Suddenly he caught sight of both his acquaintances entering the garden from the forest. His shock was overwhelming, frightful, abysmal. He felt as though even the music had been affected, taken aback, reduced in volume by half, as if a kind of icy breath had drifted over all things and people nearby.

The women came closer. He was unable to find the strength to look at them. They sat down at a table about twelve paces away.

He was regaining his senses. The music radiantly surged once more to the heights, and his eyes rested on their faces.

Their resemblance to one another, though remote, was uncanny. Some-thing palpitating and delicate, demonically ethereal veiled both their pallid visages, something he had not seen in a woman's face before. But from the face of the younger woman in blue it glared, thundered incomparably more powerfully . . . She was about twenty years old, tall, slim. Pretty? Something too chilling emanated from her too pale, thin, yet entirely classically formed features, predatory and yet affectionate, horrifying in their spectral ghastliness and ferocity and also — an inhuman, a superhuman, tenderness. Perhaps she was more than pretty — in other words, to the ordinary eye she was not beautiful — every magnificent beauty is darkened by her own excessive splendour.

Yet none of the marvellous peculiarities of her face could explain the devastating and eerie impression she imparted —
— —

They did not look at him and seemed not to be paying attention to anything else around them, confusion, fear even, so apparent in the face of the lady in red. They conversed very little and quietly; even when the music died down, Sider could not hear their voices.

Finally, the older woman's eyes regarded him. She said something to her companion. Now their conversation became livelier . . . and then the younger of the two looked intently at Sider for a long time, for an almost indecent length of time. He was the first to avert his eyes, as they had grown dim and his head had started to spin. After a while he raised them again — Her eyes were still fixed on him, and the look was so ghastly it was as though they were made of glass. He kept hold of himself. "This calls for a staring match!" he said to himself and did not look away. After a good two minutes She lowered her eyes and slowly concealed Her face with the palm of Her hand — —

He exhaled deeply; exquisite pleasure flooded his soul. "She has some feelings for me, that is certain! . . . But clearly She is very eccentric, to the highest degree, no doubt. Maniacal even? Ugh! On what am I basing this judgement except the fact that She stared at me for an unusually long time? Perhaps Her eyes really are made of glass? Ugh! Her behaviour generally does not indicate blindness, though surely this enigmatic creature had some purpose in mind when She glared at me. If She was trying to intoxicate me, She succeeded — but don't forget, lassie, that besides my senses, which You have hypnotised, I also have a will, and it is forever vigilant."

He had been entirely unaware that something was happening around them, that all the patrons had become somehow subdued, alarmed, feverishly talking among themselves, albeit in hushed tones, forming small huddles at each table, that a crowd had gathered at the entrance to the garden. Everyone's eyes were directed only at the table where the strange ladies were sitting.

The music started up again, yet so haltingly and out of tune it was as if the musicians were distracted. The women were no longer conversing. Confusion and fear now increasingly marked the face of the elder of the two. She grew paler, quivering noticeably, constantly looking around. Only then did Sider find the public's behaviour conspicuous . . .

That's when the lady in blue stood up, uttered several words to Her companion with a smile, bowed politely and proudly, and walked away quickly in the direction of the forest. Reaching the gate, She turned around and again fixed Her gaze on Sider, now for just a moment, but how telling! As if it were acknowledging him, commanding, alluring and promising, caressing, threatening. —

"What should I do?" Sider said to himself. "Run after Her, introduce myself to Her? I absolutely lack the courage for that now. But what if I don't see Her again? Nonsense! She won't leave, after all I mean something to Her . . . Or maybe I should —?"

He watched as She walked out the garden — and how the crowd by the gate parted almost too rapidly before Her . . . "Ah, now I know! She is a lady of very high standing, a duchess perhaps? a princess? or maybe even a sovereign? No, I cannot run after Her as if chasing a harlot . . . For that matter, it's always more shrewd for a man to be nonchalant towards a woman. She'll come to me, She'll turn up again somewhere where I will also happen to be — of this I feel quite certain."

For a long time his eyes were fixed on the forest thickets into which She had disappeared. Then it occurred to him : "Well, I can at least speak to the other lady; I get the impression she's not too highbred. I'll find out what I need from her."

He cheered up at once, but when he glanced around he could not see the other woman either.

He was suddenly seized by a frightful, half-joyful, half-terrifying restlessness. He ran out of the garden. He noticed that everyone was now discussing something all the more passionately and loudly, but he was unable to understand any of what was being said.

•

Several days passed. He renewed his inquiries and learnt that the older woman had been staying at a hotel in Cortona for three weeks, having signed in as Mrs Errata S., rentier — she was by all accounts a wealthy widow — and that on Monday she had suddenly departed, leaving her belongings behind in her room. He discovered nothing about her companion. Although many people had seen Her on Sunday in the company of Mrs S., what they said of Her was so oddly evasive and nebulous Sider did not know what to make of it.

He spent his entire days scampering around on the surrounding mountains, consumed by a demonic desire. Then on 16 June he received a telegram that provided a categorical imperative for him to leave Cortona : his entire fortune was at risk.

Though seething with rage, something told him it was a good idea to put an end to this adventure of his. He resolved to return to Cortona as soon as possible. He got everything ready for departure, which he'd set for the following day at nine in the morning.

He got up at around eight, opened the shutters. It was a magnificent, resplendent day, already hot for that hour! As if refreshed by sleep, the mountains towered up towards the dark blue sky more powerfully than ever before. Stag's Head was the nearest, the highest, the most beautiful. He had walked up it two days before, all the way to the glacier beneath its highest rocky horns, hoping foolishly to set eyes on Her there in reality as he had seen Her there in his dream. It was to no avail.

He gazed at the mountain for a long time, bidding it farewell. He was just turning away his eyes when . . . — he shuddered.

At a height of about 900 metres, at the very point where the lower forest gave way to rocky ground, he spotted two dots, blue and red . . . Frantically he grabbed his field glasses. It was the women, slowly ascending.

Without deliberating he threw on some clothes, seized his walking stick, and rushed out the door.

"No departing today," he said to himself decisively, practically flying towards the restaurant. "If I incur huge financial losses, so be it, it's not as if my life were at stake. Whatever awaits me up there is much more important, just as the soul is more important than the wallet. Despite my timidity, I must, must speak with them! But will I find them there? Certainly; they no doubt intend to go to the summit of Stag's Head, otherwise they wouldn't be so high up so early in the day. I cannot miss them — there's only one path up the mountain, and even though it forks beneath the summit, one trail is clearly visible from the other. I'll probably catch up with them right on the peak. They are way ahead of me, but they're women. It's normally an eight-hour climb, if I put my mind to it I can make it in five."

He was beside himself with excitement and joy. Once in the forest he took off at a gallop up the gently rising trail and continued apace with short breaks for almost an hour until he was out of the forest, 800 metres above the valley. The path now wound steeply up the rocky slope, dotted with patches of mountain scrub. Flustered, he looked upwards to see if he could catch a glimpse of the coloured spots. He could not. He climbed higher and higher, passing the point where he had seen them from his room an hour and a half before . . .

"Just another 100 metres up to that overhanging rock! The slope is too curved at this point for me to be able to get a good view. Up there I'll surely see them — I don't think they should be more than 600 metres above me. It's so hot, I'm more soaked than if I'd been drenched by rain, and I'm shamefully tired to boot. I'll rest once I get up there; they can't get away from me, if it's really even them."

Reaching his destination — and sure enough he spotted them not more than 600 metres above him. He lay down, contented, lit a cigar, and fantasised blissfully about what might be waiting for him on the summit. Twenty minutes later he was once again ascending rapidly.

They disappeared from his sight. When he saw them again, he was surprised at how high up they were; it looked as though they'd almost reached the glacier. "No, they couldn't have climbed almost 1000 metres in half an hour. In the Alps, heights and distances are often deceptive!"

Again they vanished. He walked up the steep, relatively safe path as quickly as possible for the better part of an hour. He couldn't see them now, and though this was not out of the ordinary, it exasperated him to no end. He reached the point where the path forked in two, rested for a moment, and hurried up the left path.

He was about 800 metres below the summit. He was walking swiftly for it had occurred to him that they might go down the opposite slope, to the hamlet on the other side of the mountain. "Come what may I'll surely catch up with them at the top, or at least I'll catch sight of them, they won't have been able to get too far down."

When he saw them a little while later, he was overcome with joy! With his field glasses he could clearly make out that they were still about 200 metres below the ridge. Victory! Not only could he now distinguish the characteristic pallor of their cheeks, but also some of their features.

He slackened his pace. Once more they disappeared from view, and for the first time that day the sun also vanished, dropping behind a small cloud. A cold wind blew sharply from the glacier, howling menacingly . . . Then suddenly Sider heard a cry from above, very faint, yet quite audible . . .

"An accident!" He froze, stupefied, yet a moment later he was off at a trot. "Has one of them fallen? Or have they been waylaid? Ah! Some good may come of it yet! At least I'll show them that they need me!"

Although his legs felt leaden, he kept running upwards. But in a short while he stopped, stupefied once more.

Several hundred paces to the right, on the other path, he saw the lady in red running down so swiftly it was a wonder she didn't trip and fall . . .

"What's happened? Might I be of assistance?" he shouted.

The woman stopped in her tracks — — she cried out once more and continued running. His repeated shouts to her had no effect; she didn't stop, she didn't look back.

"The other lady must have plummeted — She! . . . and Her companion is running down to get help . . . But why didn't she at least turn to me for assistance? Clearly she was totally deranged with terror. Whatever the case, the mere chance that something untoward may have befallen Her is enough — I have no other choice — upwards!"

The path led higher and higher. The clouds in the sky grew in number and size, thickening, growing more grey and brown; the wind blew colder and louder, howling all the more. Running, Sider reached the spot where they had recently rested and slumped down, feeling he'd collapse if he didn't lie down. But in a minute he was back on his feet. He shouted several times. No answer. Or was there? . . . Yes — But was it not coming from below? He looked around. Another barely audible cry. And then, through his field glasses, he saw the lady in red once again, far, far below him, standing, waving her arms, waving her shawl. She seemed to be beckoning him. He stood there, indecisive, confused. "What does it all mean? Does she want me to help her look for someone, or something? Or is she warning me? About robbers? Is it possible that her guide had been a bandit disguised as a woman? . . . Silly questions! Should I heed her wishes? Yet — She must be close; a chance to replace the uncertain with the certain . . . maybe the woman below is just acting on some foolish impulse, female apprehension . . . Even so — at least she knows something, while I know nothing —"

Again the cries from the depths below reached his ears — and made up his mind for him. He started back down. All at once he heard louder cries, this time from above :

"Here, up here!"

He looked up. At the very edge of the glacier about 50 metres below the summit he saw — Her. She wasn't moving, just a blue dot, even with his field glasses he couldn't tell if She were sitting, lying down, or standing upright. But what he saw was enough. He ran up the path, taking no heed of the renewed cries from below.

A hundred metres further up — the blue figure remained immobile. Fifty — now it disappeared behind a crag — a minute later it emerged again and quickly continued upwards.

"What's going on here? She probably isn't injured, at least not seriously, otherwise She would head down. Perhaps She's made up her mind to reach the summit despite a light injury. No doubt this demonic woman is awfully headstrong. No matter, I can be all the more of service to Her — given all that's happened, it would not be considered intrusive for me to join Her."

She reached the summit plateau and vanished from his eyes when he was still 50 metres below it. He had to rest. He'd never felt so exhausted. He had completed the climb in record time. His watch showed noon. The sun hid itself completely behind a vast, thick layer of cloud.

Finally he stood on the mountaintop. He did not see an enchanting panorama, he only saw a thin figure about 400 paces further on against a blue patch of sky, as if it were a diaphanous shadow, an outline barely discernable, spectral, moving towards the highest of the cone-shaped rocks towering another 150 metres or so above the high plateau. She clearly intended to climb that as well. Three days before, Sider had walked to its base. He'd not had time to go any higher since it would have meant getting home in the middle of the night, so he'd given up grudgingly, even though he knew from guidebooks to the Alps how dangerous it was. A very narrow path wound its way up the cone-shaped rock, coiling round it like a whip, yet in places it almost vanished among the virtually sheer rock faces.

"At least now I'll make the climb, and with Her," he thought and followed after Her as quickly as possible. To his astonishment, however, She pressed on, without looking back, at an even faster pace than his. He started running over snow, glacial boulders, and sloughs. But she had already disappeared behind the first of the cone-shaped rocks.

Running, he reached the same spot. Hardly had he placed his foot on the steeply rising path when he was overcome by something indescribable. A recollection, a monster emerging from the depths like the gruesome Leviathan from the dreaded abyss of the ocean; . . . and though it immediately submerged again, it long reverberated in his soul. "How horribly familiar this place seems to me . . . I've seen it before, I've been here before, a long time ago — and something immense transpired here . . . When, oh when? Surely it was in a dream; in my dreams I used to see Her here, too, this much is clear — but what is a dream except the continuation of reality, or is reality the continuation of the dream? The dream is the depth of the waking state to which we are blind when awake, and the falsehood and deceptiveness and illogical nature of the dream — merely the concentration of all the rays of this World-Phantasm."

He was now in the grips of a dread so powerful it nearly drowned out his desire. He felt inclined to turn back. A chill wind blew from the lowering sky, all the time growing colder, its bellowing becoming an increasingly high-pitched howl, as if spirits were warning him, lamenting his fate. Snow started to fall, becoming heavier and heavier, as if intending to form his burial mound. Spurred on now only by momentum, he dragged himself onwards, and a faintness that was as much physical as it was mental weighed him down.

There was a constant danger of falling into the ever-growing chasm below. Progress was very slow, but he had already passed the halfway point.

Then, having just avoided plummeting to his death, he was overcome with such despondency he stopped and abruptly decided to head back.

And then he caught sight of Her once more. Only about 60 paces ahead of him. So suddenly . . . She waved him onwards, beckoning him, and disappeared where the path curved behind a rock.

Surrendering his will, Sider staggered after Her, after Her. He did not know whether he was asleep or awake, or whether he was in the netherworld. "Even if She's the devil incarnate," he whispered to himself dully, "and that could easily be the case, — I must, I must."

He reached the bend — and froze in fright. The path before him was no more : a small rock fall had torn it away. Something resembling a path continued about a metre and a half further on. It required a leap! It was impossible to walk around the rift as above and below there was nothing but smooth, sheer rock face. A leap might succeed, though it was much more likely to end with a plunge into the chasm about 30 metres below, for the path onto which the foot should land was so narrow there wasn't even room for the other foot, and there was nothing whatsoever to grab hold of on the other side. Salto mortale. He was now so exhausted his legs were shaking, and when a more forceful gust of wind might knock him off his feet and send him plummeting — could he dare attempt such a leap . . . ?

He stood there, unable to make up his mind, his heart pounding terribly. Fear struggled savagely with shame, with pride. She had done it! He could not see Her, and certainly She had not plummeted into the abyss — he would have heard a scream, or at least the thud of a body below. A woman had pulled it off, and he, a man, should —? He found the thought unbearable!

He took as much of a run-up as the place allowed, but stopped at the edge of the precipice. He shuddered and realised he didn't have the courage . . . ; he knew the leap would result in death. He looked down, his limbs turned to ice. What was it again that screamed at him so transcendentally, so eerily from the abyss?

The struggle was over. In shame he retraced his steps like a whipped dog. To cheer himself up he resolved to make the leap no matter what on another occasion, when his body would be in better shape to serve his intentions. He had only gone twenty paces when an appalling, ghastly cry rang out from somewhere above :

"You coward! You wimp!"

He saw Her at the very top of the cone-shaped rock. He seemed to be able to make out Her infernal countenance, burning with fury and hate — —

"You scoundrel, vile abomination, your cowardice is as great as your wretchedness, you dog, you dog!" — the Valkyrie-like voice roared once more, and the blue apparition vanished. —

Under different circumstances such affronts from a woman he worshipped would have prompted Sider to attempt the impossible, even to go and meet his death voluntarily. Yet absolute exhaustion, an unnatural dread, and the weather now made all action unthinkable. Numbly he descended as far as the glacier and lay down . . . Snow was still falling heavily, monster-like clouds had descended and were hurtling towards Sider with terrifying speed from all sides like a hydra. All of a sudden he was enveloped in the thickest fog.

"What now?" he said to himself indolently after a moment. "I suppose it's my duty to wait here for Her to start back down. But do I dare to stand before Her? . . . She might take the path on the other side of Stag's Head. But who could be sure of anything in this situation? She's the devil, no doubt She's expert in magic, She has no need of a miserable wretch like me . . . Brr, how cold it is here, and I can't even see two steps in front of me! Going down is impossible right now, even though the path is no longer very dangerous. Nothing to be done about it, I'll have to wait it out until the fog clears. How unbearable it all is!"

He waited, calling out often, hoping to alert the weird mountaineer to his presence on Her way down. Nothing. It took two hours for the fog to lift — flashes of sun but not a single living soul to be seen anywhere — the deepest silence. Slowly, not thinking about anything, Sider dragged his feet down the mountain. The stars were already starting to shine as he entered the garden restaurant like a sleepwalker.

•

Early the next morning he went to the hotel to inquire after Mrs Errata S. He learnt that she had returned to Cortona two days before, and on the following day she had gone for a walk in the forest behind the restaurant, as was her custom, and did not appear again until late afternoon in a most peculiar state; and thereupon she settled her entire bill without further ado and left Cortona for good before the day was out. —

Sider spent the morning on the slopes of Stag's Head, hoping in trepidation that he might see Her . . . That afternoon he departed.

3

The one day postponement of his departure was enough to cause Sider to lose almost his entire fortune. He was forced to give up his independence, to work, to struggle against destitution. And this went on for a long, long time . . .

Even so, She filled his soul entirely for many years. He loved Her — absent, unknown, phantasmagorical — wildly. The horror and flights of superstition soon left his stout heart, transforming into simple love and desire. The mysterious nature of the whole affair only served to kindle his feelings. He became firm in his conviction that his beloved was an extraordinarily unique woman, a genius, eccentric to the point of being half-mad, and that all Her actions had been governed solely by a mysteriously engendered love for him, that while the motives behind Her entire course of action were momentarily shrouded in impenetrable mystery, there was no reason to view them any differently than a detective does a seemingly inexplicable crime.

At first, he would often have the urge to set off for Cortona, and would have done so if external circumstances had not always prevented it, making it all the harder as the years went by — —

But as time passed his love waned, as do all things; his memories faded, absorbed by grim reality. Eventually he could hardly remember the incident at all . . . Oddly, the Mysterious Woman would appear more and more often in his dreams. Yet after ten years even these dreams petered out — —

Then his material situation changed. He received a small inheritance and said to himself : "I'll try my luck at gambling; I'll sacrifice half my inheritance, but not one heller more!" Within three days he'd made more money in gambling houses than a normal person earns in a lifetime.

He could now leave for the Alps whenever he wished — but the whole affair was so far behind him he was unable to stir himself to action. — He resolved to devote his life to thought and creativity, and at the same time to live it up just a little. The two, however, are incompatible, for every higher aspiration entails asceticism. And fate had ordained a different path for wretched Sider than for him to become a conqueror of the realm of the Spirit. Hedonism soon gained supremacy over all noble pursuits, slowly pressing him closer and closer to the ground. But debauchery can never fully satisfy even the lowbrow, let alone a spirit reaching for the heights. Sider was in the grips of over-satiation and overexcitement at one and the same time; the emptiness of his soul became more profound, calling on something to fill it.

•

Two years passed from the time he had acquired a new fortune. He was now forty.

He was walking down the busiest street of a metropolis far north of the Alps. It was a late, as yet sweltering evening in August. The shimmer of electric streetlamps made the last remains of a red sunset almost imperceptible. His soul was immersed in a deep sleep; once again it dwelled in the Alps. "I wonder what She's up to? What was She up to before? Will I ever lay eyes on Her again? . . . It was so magnificent and glorious . . ." Sublime tears fell from his eyes. "Is it possible that I might never see Her again? . . ."

Suddenly Her image burst from his soul like a flash of lightning so horrifically vivid that for a moment he doubted whether it was a phantasm or reality . . . He shook violently, stopped and

— —

— suddenly he saw Her in reality! Just like that first time in the ravine, though now Her magical countenance passed by even closer, almost touching his cheek. But She did not glance at him.

Later he was surprised that he hadn't sunk to his knees, that he'd been able to hold himself up by grabbing onto a streetlamp . . . How long had he stood there? . . . Three seconds or three minutes? . . . He'd hurried after Her, driven by blind instinct. He could not locate Her in the crowd.

"What was it?" he said to himself afterwards as he trod along aimlessly. "Hallucination or reality? At the very moment when my entire soul seized Her whole being, I also saw Her with my eyes. Was it just my overly vivid vision condensing into matter? Or is it the other way round : the reason I thought about Her so intensely before was because She was close by, and after so many years She was drawing nearer and nearer to me once again? . . . To hell with all these theories! If not a hallucination, was it really Her? After all, some faces are astonishingly similar . . . But no, no one else resembles Her, I know that with absolute certainty! But — She didn't appear to have aged at all in twelve years . . . But — haven't there been quite a few cases of people who seem not to age? Ach, this is going nowhere! I must do something!"

He now came to that street daily, as it had become a shrine for him, at that same time, as well as at other times of day. Frantically he scoured the entire town and sought Her out in other ways, too. Without the least result. Yet his faded love had flared up once more, and more forcefully than before. His soul burst into flames, its void avidly filled with mystical light, the past resurrected from its grave. For a second time he fell in love. With what exactly? . . . Time, which is but the unfurling of thought, flows slowly, ever so slowly, more than enough of it in Eternity. And the Sublime creeps towards every human, every animal, sometimes as a pleasant tingling sensation, at others in the form of the greatest delight; more commonly it is as the most intense horror, creeping closer and closer like a tiger silently on the prowl . . . , so that the people of today, who are animals through and through, may one day become — God.

He did not find Her. At the end of October he left for Cortona. He stayed for one week only. He did not see Her, even though he climbed all the way to the place where the path was broken. He would not have been inclined to make the leap even had She beckoned him with open arms. His soul was as dead as decayed nature at All Hallows, unstirred by the slightest tremor of light the whole time he was there . . . Even the search for the Unknown Woman and Her companion remained fruitless. "Home, home! That's where I saw Her, maybe that is where I'll find Her!"

He did not. Nothing whatsoever transpired during the winter. He worked and got drunk, he got drunk and worked, and in the end he just got drunk. Winter passed, spring timorously crept in, and for a second time Sider's strange love receded from his mind.

•

One early evening in April he was standing in front of a shop window. Its back was lined with a mirror, and in front of it were pictures of mountain scenery, one of Cortona among them. His entire soul became absorbed in the contemplation of Stag's Head. He felt as though he were climbing it again, he could see the blue and red dots as he had done on that beautiful, that dreadful, day — and then Her on that monstrous, severed path . . . — and suddenly, with terrible clarity, he saw Her face in the mirror at the back of the window! Her! Her eyes eerily staring into his.

He turned round with lightning speed. Two men and two young women were standing behind him, and there was as little resemblance between their round chirpy red faces and Hers as there can possibly be between human faces. Not a single other human being was in the vicinity.

"A hallucination? That would be the first time in my life. But no : I must also have been hallucinating that evening in August, and even in Cor–, but how nonsensically our illogical mind immediately starts to blow things out of proportion! In August it was something else; it could have been real, just as surely as it could have been an illusion — and in Cortona, at least in the garden, She was seen by almost a hundred people. It does not follow that having seen Her in reality it's impossible for me to see Her as a hallucination at another time. If, for example, this bust of Dante in the shop window were to appear before my eyes on my bed sheets while I was gripped by fever, it would not mean that the one here does not exist in reality . . . So I'm being visited by Her phantom. Is it because — She is dead? Did She die on that very evening in August? Could it be that I was suddenly compelled to contemplate Her so intensely at that moment, and thus also to see Her with my eyes, because at that very minute Her soul was leaving Her body? It's been known to happen. All this is just mere conjecture, though, nothing scientific. The worst of it is the uncertainty. I feel it could even turn to madness . . . Hah! How horridly those abysmal eyes stared at me again in the mirror just now! As if I were actually seeing them once again — —"

He rightly felt the situation was becoming extremely perilous. For a third time his passion had ignited — without the prospect of fulfilment — he had become Tantalus — condemned always to lose his beloved the moment She appeared to him . . . But the hallucinations had made matters more complicated and had added something new, something horrifying. No matter where he was, he saw only Her, Her, Her and Her terrible mirrored glare, piercing his eyes and soul with a funereal chill. Now its recurrence, its repetition, was horrid : even the constant intrusion of a single, entirely banal word into the mind can drive one insane. The matter at hand was decidedly not mundane. This was not the sweet face of a lover, but the transcendentally terrible visage of a dragon. And almost every night She visited his dreams, hideous, stifling, chaotically maniacal dreams, a diabolical gorgon forever sharing his bed. On the verge of succumbing to the terror of it all, he felt himself slipping into "superstition"; but his bright, logical mind put up a powerful defence against the temptation of seeing in it anything "supernatural." Almost all of today's educated men are "unsuperstitious" in their minds, while in their hearts they're as superstitious as old women. Sider was the opposite : his sceptical intellect allowed for the possibility that anything may exist in the world; his intellectualised inner being, however, indomitably denied the potential existence of anything spectral. He still believed that the Mysterious Woman was as real a being as he was himself. The question for him now was : is She still alive, or is She dead? And this uncertainty was unhinging his mind, just as the ghastly turmoil of dark emotions was doing to the whole of his inner being.

•

Then something happened which changed this awful state of affairs. On 22 May he was walking down a bustling street in a different part of the city than the previous August. Once again it was evening, but the red sunset still blazed in full splendour. Exceptionally, he was in a fairly cheery mood. Then all of a sudden he saw Her. Facing the other way, She was just crossing the street a few paces ahead of him. It was Her! She was well lit by the crisp red sky! Even the two moles on the left side of her face were visible. This time his fright was not as great — and immediately he headed towards Her. Yet at that very moment She stopped next to a police officer at the intersection and spoke to him.

Backing off a little, Sider waited. Some time elapsed before the police officer gave Her a parting salute. Sider rushed after Her as She hurried away. Suddenly She disappeared behind an electric streetcar. He started running, and was almost run over by an automobile hidden by the streetcar. A moment later, having recovered from the shock, he could no longer see Her. He rushed into the throng of cars and people where She had just disappeared. His entire soul transformed into eyes. Futile. In a desperate rage, just about to break down in tears, he remembered the police officer.

He ran up to him wildly. "Did a woman dressed in blue, very pale, with little moles right here, speak to you just now?"

"Well yes, and what's it to you?"

"She did!" he shouted joyfully. "So She was real?"

"Hmm — hmm," muttered the policeman, his eyes bulging out of his head in an expression of severity and stupidity.

"And what did She want?"

"What business is that of yours?"

"Oh, dear sir, but it is my business!" And he gave the policeman three ducats. They served as ample proof that it was indeed his business. He learnt that the lady had inquired how to get to Cliff Street, that She had readily told him She was a stranger in the city and had been living in that street for several days but was at that moment having trouble locating it. — In answer to Sider's question if his heart had felt odd when he looked at Her, the policeman shook his head with his mouth agape and gravely nodded his head in pity as the generous gentleman walked off

— —

Sider knew one thing with absolute certainty : when the automobile was hurtling towards him, Her supercelestial eyes had rested on his for an instant, though no longer ghastly, but kind, smiling, alluring, kissing, sonorously inviting. He was enlivened by the certitude that his Radiance still dwelled on the earth. He now saw everything in the most beauteous earthly light. "My love is alive! She is weird in the extreme, mystical powers at Her command, as is my love for Her! And She loves me, loves me!" His faith now resided in these three things : "She will now finally provide the purpose I have lost; She will fill my emptiness; She will give me life!" Never before had he felt so happy, so alive, so sprightly, so divine.

Over the days that followed he expended more energy trying to find Her in Cliff Street than on anything he had ever done in his life. He conducted his search with no care for pride or shame. He searched every house in the street, systematically, from cellar to attic, indeed from cellar to dovecote, and he also visited many apartments and asked every person in the street if they knew anything about the pale lady with moles. Eventually, the local boys shouted at him "lunatic!" "moron!" — Cliff Street was long; it took its name — incidentally — from the limestone cliffs that towered along its length. It took him three days to search the entire street, and still he came up with nothing, nothing . . .

By the evening of the third day he had covered the street's length. Only one small house remained, standing apart from all the rest some two hundred paces further on. He could see that it was impoverished, almost black, dilapidated. "Surely She cannot be living there, but just to be thorough, now that I've searched everywhere else, I'll take a look there as well."

The back of the little edifice leant directly against a high cliff, jagged, as if pieces of it had broken off. The house had two floors and was dismally derelict. Standing before it, Sider now regarded it in the evening twilight and froze with fear. It looked exactly like, in fact it was identical to, the mysterious cottage in Cortona by the entrance to the ravine with the rock suspended above it like the sword of Damocles, as if its doppelgänger . . .

He sat on the baulk opposite the house for half an hour. "Only here, here could She live . . . Ugh! Mere coincidence! I'm starting to see ghosts in everything! I need to free myself of this once and for all! For — spectres and the belief in them contradict the Will! Not the 'external world' — that is always tame and subservient to it — : It is spectres that kill the Will! Time to have a look!"

It was now night. Sider took a step towards the house, he looked it over once more — his whole body shook . . . "No, not today! I won't manage. My legs are shaking so much I can hardly stand. Cursed matters of physiology! Tomorrow, the morning will be more favourable!"

He returned home, lay down on his bed. — Without even knowing how, he suddenly found himself in front of the mysterious little house. Automatically he entered. He briskly walked through the hallway on the ground floor, his steps absolute and sure, without even having to light a match, as if walking through his own house. He went to the upper floor, which was also in complete darkness. He extended his hand — and felt a handle. He found himself in a room, which in contrast to the ragged exterior of the house was furnished with striking elegance, by all appearances the bedroom. The full moon glaring at him through the window nearly dazzled him; what poured from the moon into his soul was not light, but the words: "Don't you know me? Ah, you know me well! Try to remember!" He took a better look around. He saw — rocks, bricks, chunks of wood scattered over the carpets — and the conjugal bed in the corner smashed to pieces, a large boulder protruding from its wreckage, embedded in the floor. He drew nearer, inquisitive and absolutely calm, and saw a young woman in a nightshirt amid the wreckage. Her face — covered in blood, her nose crushed, both legs draped in blood. "What happened here?" he said to himself; "it seems I should know . . . , how witless I am today!" He was trying to solve the mystery as coolly as he would an ordinary rebus. In the meantime the girl had begun to move weakly, moaning, but without opening her eyes. Suddenly he felt a cold draft on his head; it was coming from above. He looked up : a hole in the roof; several stars and the silhouette of the cliff peered through the opening. "Well, well, look at that . . . ; but I still don't know anything, though first I should get this injured woman to a doctor." He grabbed hold of her and then felt his hands somehow sinking disgustingly into her flesh. He looked at his fingers, they were coated with red-brown dust, reeking pungently. "Well, well!" he said to himself calmly and vigorously squeezed her thigh. It crumbled into lumps of repugnant stuff. And then a dark horror flared within him — at once the moon's radiance transformed into a windstorm of light that hurtled towards him, intensifying into the most frightful black hurricane, — the silently motionless hurricane of Eternity, and at that moment the woman opened her eyes. — It was Her! . . . And a monstrous, ghastly thought thundered in him, a thought from the very heart of insane All-Mystery — a mere waft of this thought could rip apart the pathetic human soul more effectively than a cannon ball could a spider's web — —

But Sider was not yet destined to quit his second of His Life eternal, to which the microbe calling itself "human being" gives the appellation life. At the last moment an alien, providential power flung his soul out of the reach of the Most Terrible into the sphere of superficiality and blindness that is known as the waking state. He saw the table lamp by his bedside, saw himself in the wall mirror, and he raised his body up from the pillows, his hair standing on end, his face white as the sheets.

•

On the following morning he entered the house. When he closed the front door behind him he stood in complete darkness. He struck a match, nearby was a door; he stood in front of it, listening.

There was a profound silence. Suddenly he felt as though something were churning inside him . . . He continued to stand there listlessly — for a long time, for a short time, he didn't know. Then he heard a weak, very weak rustle from inside, as though made by shuffling steps coming from far off. The rustling grew louder, the steps long drawing near, as though an enormous number of rooms lay concealed behind the door. Overcome with horror, he wanted to flee, when suddenly a dreadful laugh rattled from inside, transfixing him to the spot. And very slowly, like the hands on a clock, the door opened, and just as slowly, a woman holding a burning candle shuffled through it. Her face left him dumbstruck. It seemed to be two hundred years old, as if belonging to a corpse, yet this was not the only thing he found astonishing — —

She shone the light at him, and again the inhuman laugh rattled. "Hoy there, handsome laddie, don't be afraid, don't be afraid! I know you, I know why you've come, I've been expecting you. You've come to see the lady in blue, haven't you, eh, eh?"

"Yes, the one with the two little moles — is She here?"

"She was here, stayed here for a whole week, nice of a lady like that to remember Old Barbora again. She left yesterday, but, hee hee, She left a photograph with a few words for you, wrote them Herself, handsome laddie, wrote them Herself, hee hee!"

"For me? How do you know it's for me — —"

"Hee hee, She described you to me, though no need to, no need! Even if She hadn't, I would've known! Old Barbora knows everything."

"Then She is — alive?"

"Hee hee, everything is alive, silly boy! So here you go, take it."

She took an envelope out of the pocket of her apron and handed it to him. He read his name on it, opened it. The portrait resembled the original, breathtakingly, incredibly, and on the other side he read : "Meet me on Stag's Head in June! Orea."

Orea! . . . Where had he heard that sweet name before? . . . Suddenly he had the feeling that he had whispered it himself at some point in the past and — it had been here, in this ghastly house . . .

"She loves you, laddie," the old crone grunted and laughed, "but take care that the tigress doesn't tear you apart with Her love. You whipped Her brutally, and She hasn't forgotten, hasn't forgotten."

"What are you talking about? When did I —? I did what to Her —? In a dream —?"

"Of course in a dream. Everything's a dream, hee hee."

"She wants to take revenge on me?"

"She wants to love you, but She knows She won't be able to until you've been punished, until accounts have been settled between you two. Go now, laddie, you've heard enough, go meet your destiny, your destiny, hee hee."

"Wait! Before I go, can you show me the upper floor?"

"But what's to see there? The boulders were cleared away long ago, long ago."

"Boulders? How do you know about them? Am I asleep or have I gone mad?"

"Asleep and mad, laddie, and awake as well, and of sound mind you are! Every human is all that. Now go!" — And very slowly she turned to leave.

"Please, before you leave, tell me, who is this Orea?!" he cried out, grabbing her by the shoulder with one hand and placing a pile of ducats into her palm with the other.

"You ask too much, laddie, too much! Wait three years, then you'll see! Put away your little flakes of gold! What good are they to me? Hee hee hee!"

With a terrifying sluggishness she trudged back to the chamber. And Sider, his soul transformed into chaos and yet so full of joy, ran out of that darkest night to be dazzled by the full radiance of the morning sun.

He remained standing in front of the house. He could not see, hear, think. For how long? . . . Finally he was roused by a blow to the face.

"Loony! Idiot! Nitwit!" only now he heard the shouting of the boys forming a wide circle around him. One of them had just struck him in the head with a ball of horse dung. —

"Was this all a dream again, as in the night?" he said to himself as he was being driven away in a hackney cab where he had found refuge from the raucous horde of pygmies hounding him. "Oh, will I ever know? But — even so — good God! . . ."

Never in his life had he been in such an agitated state as now when he put his hand into his breast pocket. "It won't be there, I'm certain of that!" he whispered to himself through chattering teeth . . . Never in his life had he done anything as slowly as now, as he opened his billfold — —

He yelled out so loudly that the coachman turned around in the driver's box . . . The staggering beauty of the perfect portrait thundered towards him; he had the distinctly ghastly impression that the real Orea was sitting opposite him. And he kissed, kissed Her sharp, most peculiar handwriting . . .

"She is alive! It was real!" he exulted with joy as they drove through increasingly lively streets. "Finally I have proof! Something real from Her! . . . But am I not dreaming even now? Yet — nonsense, to think I can't distinguish my current state of mind from a dream? It would be easier to mistake that cat over there for a zither!" He took out the portrait once more. "I still have it! — And having it means I'm richer than all the kings in the world! Oh, with this picture and this handwriting I'll be happy forever! . . . She lives! And She loves me . . . All the horrid strangeness of this my tale of romance makes it all the more beautiful and beguiling. Who can boast of such a fantastical, poetic Romance as mine? . . . All that is murky will be illuminated in June . . . Today is just 23 May — I can't wait . . . I can't bear all this happiness . . . All is good and beautiful. To Cortona, Orea, my dear Orea! — —"

4

On the first of June at two o'clock in the afternoon Sider was already disembarking from the train at the station in Cortona. It was one of those rare, ghastly days at the end of an ageing spring when the entire sky is covered by a single dense cloud, not thick enough to completely obscure the sun, not thin enough to allow it even a faint radiance; the sun appeared like a slightly brighter cloud. The sky a desert, the earth, a hue indescribably hideous, a desert, everything solemnly, sultrily, chokingly, appallingly dead. Awful in the plains, even more awful is such a day in the mountains.

"Brr, what a pleasant welcome from Stag's Head," he shivered "it's glaring at me like the corpse of someone who's died of horror. What is it saying to me today? . . . What monstrosity has flown so chillingly from it into my soul?" He had an inexplicable feeling that the joy of the previous days had evaporated, that permanent dread and misfortune would take its place, that he was standing on the threshold of a new era.

He checked into a hotel. Tired from the journey, he lay down and fell asleep. He did not wake until nightfall, his mood subdued and chaotic.

"Today — I'll just go to the garden restaurant," he decided. "Tomorrow — I'll call on the black house in the ravine. And the day after — Stag's Head. Yes, that's the plan."

In the garden he caught sight of the doctor from Cortona with whom he'd conversed on several occasions during his stay the previous year, an intelligent man — with that specific intelligence of doctors that, in its most important respects, is closer to idiocy than even the most extreme obtuseness — and somewhat of a pig. Sider sat down at his table; the doctor was drinking heavily and diligently, enjoying the company of his own corpulence, and he immediately diverted the conversation to the only theme that interested him.

"Today I have some news for you," said the doctor, "for over a year now Mrs Errata S. has been interned in a lunatic asylum." He named the town it was in.

Something made Sider shudder. A foreboding that a similar fate awaited him? The sense that his destiny was mystically bound up with hers? Or compassion and love? Errata was never indifferent to him, and even though his feelings towards her could not be compared to his love for Orea, there had been moments in the past when he had felt that his love for her exceeded even that for the woman whose portrait he now carried in his breast pocket.

"Really? . . . Could you give me any more details? Please!"

"Several months ago I received an official letter from the psychiatrist there," the doctor said and spat, "who is treating her. He requested I give him a medical report on her mental state. That deranged woman had told him that she'd had several consultations with me twelve years ago about her 'nervous disposition,' and she said that's when her mental illness started. I wrote back that Mrs S. suffers from dementia praecox, but this psychiatrist person did not agree with me, the idiot, and let me know, between the lines, that the one suffering from dementia praecox is more likely to be I than she. Such is the nature of some of those in our field of science, pooh!" and he poured a large glass down his throat.

"Her illness originated back then? Could you tell me anything else about it?"

"According to my dear colleague, the cretin, the cause is that this woman fell head-over-heels in love with some other female individual, but the love affair was, ha ha, most ill-fated, because the terror Mrs Errata felt for her idol outweighed any erotic pleasure she derived. But this is all nothing more than symptoms of dementia praecox, even a cretin like that should be able to see as much."

"Has Errata had relations with her beloved since the time they were seen together here?"

"How should I know, my boy? Well in fact — that idiot — ahem, said that she often saw her in ha– hallucinations. And that's just the dementia praecox again. Yes — and well — yes, she talked often about you, too. Perhaps she fell in love with you, ha ha, you can go there and marry her."

"Do you know anything more about the other one?"

"What could I know, my boy? But I know everything. Hmm, what was it I wanted to . . . people talk a lot about her round here, but it's all just old wives' tales. They say she's a —"

"Doctor, Doctor," shrieked a woman running towards them, "I beg you to come with me, quickly, my husband is dying, he fell off a cliff and his head's completely broken!"

"To hell with it!" the doctor muttered, reaching slowly for his glass. "One doesn't get a moment's respite! What an idea, falling off a cliff. And so late in the evening! Why couldn't he wait till morning to have his bit of fun?" He slowly emptied his glass. "I bet he was drunk, wasn't he?"

"Oh no, Doctor, for God's sake please hurry, maybe his life can still be saved —"

"Let go of my sleeve — you — you unsavoury person — I — what was it I wanted? Hey, waiter, my bill — tally up what I owe for today — no, for the whole week!" Standing up, he staggered noticeably. "I'm — damn it —"

Sider tossed a few gold coins on the table. "I'm paying — does that cover it?" He took hold of the doctor under his arm. "Let's go, quickly, I'll accompany you. I might be of some assistance — I studied medicine for a time."

"You — medicine, a cretin like you? Ha!"

He listed so much that Sider only just managed to keep his heavy body upright as he dragged him towards the exit.

"Could you," he made a final attempt to exploit the situation, "tell me in one word what the locals say about the mysterious lady?"

"A tramp is what! And a hallucination to boot, that is, a nexus — actually a pexus polaris, solaris in fact, — damn it all, I've forgotten everything, dementia praecox. Gaudeamus igitur —" he started shouting. Extricating himself from Sider's grasp, he staggered and fell flat on his face with an almighty crash.

Sider went off on his own with the whimpering woman to tend to the injured man. He was already dead.

•

The night was a long string of dreadful, hellish dreams. In the morning rain fell from a dark sky. At around ten o'clock Sider set out for the ravine. He was in a pathologically gloomy and agitated mood, almost to the point of skittishness. The previous day's conversation had left him with a vague feeling of horror, for which he could not satisfactorily account. "After all, that drunkard didn't tell me anything specific, besides the valuable information of Errata's whereabouts. Of Orea I know as little as ever. But he'll tell me the rest tonight — a doctor surely cannot be as drunk as that day in, day out."

On seeing the black cottage, its similarity to the house in Cliff Street, not the similarity of a twin, but that of a double, again sent a shudder through him. But here the cliff loomed directly above the house — a boulder weighing several tons threatened to fall straight down on it at any moment. "I would not want to live here," he shuddered again. It required a great surge of will for him to enter.

This time he left the door open behind him. He saw the same

hallway he'd seen before in the light of Barbora's candle. Even the door on the right was in the same place.

He stood there. He did not dare knock on the door. Silence, only the soft murmur of the rain and the increasing pounding of his heart . . . "Will I again hear steps as if coming from rooms infinitely distant, maniacally shuffling closer and closer and closer? . . ."

No. Suddenly the door opened slightly — an old woman . . . In some respects she resembled Barbora, but it wasn't her, neither her features, nor her age. Although she was very old, in her nineties by all appearances — she had nothing of the paradoxical, transcendentally animated deathliness of the old crone from Cliff Street.

"What do you want?" she asked in a voice that was still quite sonorous.

"Excuse me, what? Oh — yes, do you have a room to let?"

"Yes, yes, and not one, but two. No one wants to stay here, would you have the courage?"

"Why courage?"

"Because they say the place is haunted. And because that cliff looms right over the house. But we're not afraid, what do old people have to fear?"

"Who else lives here besides you?"

"My mother."

"You still have — a mother?"

"Yes I do, one of God's miracles it is. I don't know what she did wrong that God is taking so long to call her to Him. She's one hundred and thirty seven years old and I'm —"

"May I see her?"

"Well, if you really want to. But I wouldn't advise it, you'll be seeing her in your dreams for years to come. She's been bedridden for twenty years now, she can't move, she's blind, deaf, and doesn't talk, her throat just rattles the whole time. She simply won't die."

"Take me to her!"

She led him through the kitchen into the adjoining room, dark as nightfall. There Sider beheld — — his acquaintance from Cliff Street. She seemed to him even more horrible than before; he very nearly fainted.

Her blind eyes were fixed glassily on the ceiling, a quiet and dreadful rattle issuing without interruption from her gaping mouth . . . slowly gaining in strength, starting to resemble words — and suddenly, this was distinctly audible :

"Have you finally come, you devil's spawn? I've held on long enough to cross paths with you again, ha ha, ha ha! Be cursed, cursed, you dirty bleeding cur!"

"Jesus Christ, she's talking again after twenty years," the daughter clasped her hands together.

"Why are you cursing me?" he inquired frantically, yet firmly.

"She can't hear."

"Because you killed my daughter, you scoundrel of scoundrels, my sweet child whom I suckled. I've been waiting for you, I've waited a long time, finally I get to set eyes on you again. Be forever cursed, you Satan's miscarriage! Hah, death is already hurrying towards you, black is God's judgement! You will be crushed, crushed like her, my dear daughter —"

While uttering these words in an unnaturally powerful voice, she lurched violently, her body — no, a mere skeleton — raised itself up and then fell back again with a terrible rasping . . .

"A miracle!" her daughter dropped to her knees. "She hasn't moved her arms or spoken in twenty years, she's blind — and now before you — You, you are a murderer, go away!"

"What daughter were you talking about? I know nothing! Speak!" he said in a voice that was so commanding he almost blacked out from the effort.

Silence.

"Was it you who gave me the portrait of Orea in Cliff Street?"

Silence. "For God's sake, she's not rasping any more — she must have died!" screamed the daughter — she leaned over the bed. "She's no longer breathing!" she shrieked in a strange voice. "You murdered her, just like you did the other, you cutthroat! — Oh, my beloved mummy!" she howled unnaturally after a while.

"What 'other'? I haven't a clue . . ."

"Nor do I, but Mummy knew! God spoke through her! Get away from here, you Belial! Help, murderer!"

Reeling, Sider ran outside. "Murderer, murderer!" she screeched after him. "He killed my mother! Catch the murderer!"

But the black cottage stood on its own, the nearby lane devoid of people . . . Eventually Sider was no longer pursued by the old woman's cries.

He ran around Cortona aimlessly for some time before he was able to think more clearly. "Diabolical! Incredible! I feel as if I'm becoming more and more susceptible to the old crone's belief that I'm in the clutches of some infernal power . . . I'm beginning to feel genuine fear — and — now I really feel like — putting all this behind me and leaving this accursed nest at once. But — no! That would be cravenly rash! —"

Still he dithered. It was not his decisiveness that led to a decision.

He soon became aware that everywhere little groups of people were forming, talking excitedly. He heard the words : "Murder — Old Barbora — strangled — murderer — unknown foreigner — the police and gendarmes are now searching —"

Initially Sider found it ludicrous. But that soon passed. "Damn it all, surely I'll be arrested if they catch me now. They'd soon release me — but is that so certain? Everyone knows how the courts work. Who knows how long I'd have to spend in custody. What's more — hasn't judicial murder been committed on many an occasion? . . . The most sensible thing to do is flee as quickly as possible. But Orea? . . . I can make my way back here again — June is long. If I were to be imprisoned for longer, wouldn't that make it impossible for me to meet Her? Yes! I'll cross the border, wait until I see the newspapers report that the old woman died of natural causes, and then I'll return. I'd be certifiably insane to view that as cowardice." He looked at his watch. "A train is leaving in ten minutes. Excellent. I must hurry!"

He rushed to the hotel. Since he'd not yet unpacked his luggage he could leave without delay. The clusters of people he met on the way to the station were increasingly numerous and agitated. He, too, was extremely vexed, but since it was now in no way metaphysical this had a salutary effect on him. He caught the train on time, departed in a good mood, and happily crossed the nearby border. For the time being he was safe.

•

The mental institution where Errata was interned was near the border crossing. "I'll go there first," he decided. "I'll visit her and at the same time wait there for news from Cortona. I'll be killing two birds with one stone."

On 4 June the asylum administrators informed him that Errata was incurably mentally ill, that although her mania every now and then manifested lucida intervalla, she would often erupt into fits of rage, that the primary cause was a "poor upbringing" by eccentric parents who had inculcated her with superstitious beliefs from an early age, and that it was absolutely impossible for him to speak with her.

A few gold coins placed in the palm of one of the orderlies naturally made the absolutely impossible possible. And on that very day Sider entered Errata's cell.

She was sitting in an armchair that had been nailed to the floor, her hands bound together with rope. She was staring catatonically at the ceiling; she did not look over at Sider. His initial thought was that he'd been taken to the wrong patient. At first glance, the formerly beautiful young lady looked almost like an old woman. Her cheeks were terribly emaciated, furrowed not so much with wrinkles as with suffering, their whiteness having turned sallow — like snow in late spring; her eyes had become dull and shifty at the same time, constantly moving in a ghastly manner. Most of her hair had gone white. Yet upon closer examination he recognised her, and tenderness suffused his soul with warmth; despite everything she was still tantalisingly alluring, perhaps even more so than before, idealised by great suffering.

"My gracious lady," he began. The orderly was still standing behind him.

She looked at him, the lines on her face began to convulse, the ropes on her wrists strained, and she burst into something that at first seemed like cachinnation, but then — became a horror-stricken roar.

"Sir — it's no use, let's go," the orderly took hold of his sleeve. "I'm — whatchamacallit — responsible —"

"Who might you be," cried the bound woman, "are you my beloved, or — a ghost? No, you are my love, you shall liberate me from the clutches of these louts," — she sobbed and raised her elbow to her eyes . . . — "No, you are a ghost, for the love of Christ and Mary! You, thug, throw this man out, he's nothing more than a phantom!"

"Leave us," said Sider commandingly, and gold sparkled in the palm of the orderly. He left.

Sider cut Errata's restraints. She remained seated without moving for a long time before springing up and joyfully draping her arms around Sider's neck. "You're my saviour, you will save me from them and from — Her! . . . You have no idea of the suffering I've endured! I'm not afraid of hell, I've been there, I am there! Darling, I'm not a madwoman, I'm just losing my mind a little. These louts are the ones who really drove me mad. Although I was already deranged before I came here, it was only in my emotions, not in my intellect. Despair was causing me to lose my mind, my entire soul was fluttering like a flame in a storm, but I swear to you that my thoughts never became unhinged. I never thought I was a grain of wheat, nor do I think that now, unlike one particular scholar who never set foot on the street for fear of being pecked at by pigeons, and only that is true insanity. I have started to confuse certain concepts at times, but usually I'm in so much control of my faculties it surprises me, given all they've done to me. They held me prisoner, tied me up, flogged me until I bled, gave me ice-cold showers — hunger, inactivity, and what's worst, their stupid drivel, theories, experiments. But now I feel the hour of salvation has arrived. O my beloved, is it you, you from the garden that Sunday? I fell in love with you then, just a little, hee hee hee."

She pulled him over to the bed, pushed him down on it, and kissed him wildly. He kissed her back. He had the deceptive impression he was kissing Orea — and he'd never felt such agony, delight, glory. As if the forgotten All-Mystery were rumbling open before him in friendship. It required a strong will to pull himself together. At the same moment Errata also stirred. Her hair stood on end, her face horror incarnate. "Look, over there — Her! Orea! Again, for the sake of the living God!"

He looked to where her hand was pointing. He saw something undulating in the corner of the cell like a grey-white column of vapour, slowly taking on the appearance of a human body, and it seemed he could just about make out a face — Hers. He was suddenly seized with terror, and without knowing why he waved an arm in frantic command. The apparition vanished.

"She's gone," whispered Errata, kneeling on the floor . . .
"She doesn't want me to have you. She is — jealous — hee hee
hee — that harpy from the sea! But, laddie, in fact I do love
Her more than you. Damn it, She sure can kiss better than
you, Jack! That's why I ended up in the loony bin. Because I
said I could see Her, and they couldn't. That's why every decent
person ends up in the loony bin, because they see things others,
blind lunatics, do not see. If I had at least said I was having
'hallucinations,' hee hee, I wouldn't have ended up in the nut-
house, they might have made a doctor of me. But I was so witless I told them that what I saw was true, and this is something
these idiots cannot forgive. Since then my skin's been more
black and blue than white — look!" She lifted her skirt. It was
true.

He sat her down on the bed. "I want to live my life with you
by my side," he said sincerely. "I will protect you from people
and phantoms, or I will die with you."

"You would marry me? Just look at me! I don't even know
myself, those thugs won't even give me a hand mirror! They say
it would drive me even more insane — tell me, what's a woman
without a mirror? I know I look old, but I'm certainly younger
than you, I'm only thirty-six."

"My dear Errata, tell me what happened twelve years ago in
Cortona! Everything, including your life since! But be brief and
to the point, alright, sweetheart?"

"Yes! Now I feel quite sensible, and anyway, I would always
be a model of rationality if you were with me all the time. But
whenever one of those scoundrels walks in here — I don't know

why it is : something inside me swirls so monstrously and I start jabbering nonsense. When they don't see me, they don't realize how sensible I am, when they do see me, I can't help talking nonsense. To be fair, I can't really blame them, can I?"

"On the contrary, the only thing that one should hold against people is their stupidity. Tell me, my dear!"

Errata, now acting quite like a normal person, recalled her life, at times even joyfully and cheerily. She even used the polite form with him, though he, still shaken from Orea's recent partial appearance, listened with an exasperation he had never experienced before. "Now" — he felt — "now the terrible riddle of my life will be solved. Everything till now was only preparation for this moment."

"The first time I ever saw Her was on that wet, scarlet evening in the ravine. I was wandering around near town, entirely absorbed in dreaming, and without any warning whatsoever, so suddenly, miraculously, She was standing before me. I'd never had such a fright in my life. She asked me something completely mundane in a voice of silky thunder, like a blue evening storm speaking from afar. I answered like a fool. But She was so charming, I quickly recovered and even found the courage to offer — I don't know why — to accompany Her part of the way. She accepted with a bewitching smile, and suddenly she half-embraced me, and even though this rattled me like the kiss of a tiger, from that moment on I was in love with Her. Just a minute later we met you . . . I think I would have thrown myself into your arms upon first seeing your face if She had not touched me with her elbows . . . 'He reeled when he saw you,' I told Her, just after we had walked past you. 'He knows me, without being aware of it,' she replied coldly, 'he has a bad conscience; he is the worst scoundrel on earth.' I know for certain that Her pale face turned white as chalk, I even think I heard the ghostly throbbing of Her heart — maybe I was only hearing things — or it could have been the heart of the ancient forest — I don't know. I didn't have the courage to inquire further. Suddenly I felt more and more out of sorts. As if sensing it, She left me shortly thereafter. Oh, how relieved I was when I found myself in the garden of that restaurant among friendly people! Later we kissed the whole night long, grotesquely, weeping, and we became two monsters devouring one another.

"The second time we met was on that Sunday afternoon; oddly enough, every time I saw Her then you would show up a short while later. I was sitting at the edge of the forest, near the restaurant, reading and listening to the music. All of a sudden a shadow fell across the sun-splashed book, a shadow unfathomably black, blacker than any shadow I'd ever seen in my life. Her! But I was not startled as much as the first time : quite a few people were walking nearby, and the day was as radiant as the music. She sat down next to me sweetly and started talking about my book and literature more astutely than I had ever heard a woman speak. We sat there together for a long time, I completely narcotised — and in the end She kissed me . . . From that moment — my fate was sealed! . . . I also sucked a sweet from Her lips . . . Oh, but it felt like I had kissed death — and my love was replaced by horror . . . This has been the theme of my life ever since : love — horror, horror — love : one worse than the other. — I was grateful to Her at the time when She suggested we go to the garden together. But not even that relieved my awful anxiety — only when I saw you . . . Even so, soon She prevailed . . . I again brought you up during our conversation. She said you were a nasty sadist who had no qualms over committing an erotic murder. — Is this true?"

"Whoever loves is by default a sadist, and a masochist as well : three words to describe one and the same. But I have only expressed it in harmless ways. I have always lived more in dream than in reality. It's possible I might have a rudimentary talent for magnanimous sadism, but I have never developed it."

"She also told me something similar later, that today you are on the road to atonement, though before you were — an outright beast, that in the past She had experienced it for Herself."

"In the past? . . . Perhaps — in dreams?" he said as his heart started pounding.

"Yes — She said that everything is a dream — that eternity is a dream, and *the only sin is when one goes insane in a dream,* and this needs to be put right — She said this is the reason why all people and animals and plants and stars live, and wept while She said this. I'm certain I saw tears on Her cheeks. 'She loves him,' I said to myself and became jealous. I looked at you — and was jealous of you both . . . Though I fondly look back now at that springtime of my bizarre loves . . . Yet I was feeling all the more terrible; I didn't even notice the commotion, all those eyes fixed on Her in horror . . . And then She left me, in the most lovely way again, and I ran off to smiling meadows to keep from fainting . . . Only in the evening when I was sitting in the dining room did people ask me : 'Do you know who was sitting with you!?' — —"

"Who? Who? Who?"

"The ghost of Stag's Head! Why, you're as white as snow —"

"The ghost of — Stag's — Head?"

"Yes. She's been haunting the place for at least a hundred years! She appears only in June, usually on the summit, but every now and then even on the slopes; that was the first time the ghost had been seen down in the village, that Sunday with me. Many who have seen Her over those hundred years went insane or plummeted into the chasm because their limbs suddenly gave out . . . So that's who our beloved is, tee hee hee! . . . Don't faint —"

"It's passed!" he exhaled and slumped down onto the bed. "The most terrible thing of all is to be in love with a ghost. It's dreadful enough to fall in love with a real woman and know that she's unattainable, but a phantom — let alone some infernal harpy dragging me into a realm of blackness. The most natural thing would be to run from Her — and yet one feels compelled to crawl towards Her like a squirrel into the open jaws of a python. No wonder you went half-mad, I might go entirely insane. Ugh! Away with this! But the void of the future lies ahead of me . . . Are you aware, Errata, that — at this moment — I can hardly — see you?"

"My darling, who would know that any better than I? Perhaps I will have to be the one to hold you up . . ."

"Continue!" he convulsed like a dying man. "Oh, what an idiot I've been till now, blinded for so long by the greatest of all stupidities, which we call unsuperstitiousness. It's no wonder the soul resists the notion of spectres with all available means; the breath of a ghost kills with greater certainty than all the mitrailleuses in the world . . . It doesn't kill everyone . . . not someone who is not in love, who has not lost his mind. Fortunate are those whose mind and will remain in command, both here and in the hereafter. Mine have just flown off — but they will fly back! Continue!"

"I didn't believe it myself at first, just as none of the villains here believe it today. But what the mind does not believe, the heart does. And in the end the intellect does, too; what else is left for it to do?

"So then : why did I not leave immediately and for good on that Sunday, as my dread had resolved for me? She enticed me, as did you, sir — my dear . . .

"And then that dreadful day dawned. Early in the morning, as was my custom, I went for a walk in the forest at the foot of Stag's Head. I wished to see Her, but was afraid of doing so ten times more. The deeper I went into the forest, the greater grew my fear, until finally I abruptly turned round to run back whence I had come — and I saw Her one step ahead of me . . . I dropped to my knees. She raised me up and said with an enchanting smile : 'It seems the numbskulls here have told you all kinds of tales about me! I'm always happy to lead people by the nose. Come, climb up with me, I will explain everything to you.' She said it so commandingly that I obeyed like a puppet. She told me how in the summer She always stays in a hamlet on the other side of Stag's Head, how having heard about the legend of a young woman who haunts the mountain She had decided to reinforce the locals in their superstition, and every so often She would appear at various strange times in outlandish attire, acting so bizarrely that all scarpered before Her in horror. 'Perhaps,' She said, 'there is something appalling about my face, perhaps I wield a certain power of animal magnetism, judging by the emotions I sense I have aroused in you. But a lady as intelligent as you would not believe such ridiculous old wives' tales. Today I will show you a comedy you will not soon forget, but for that we need to climb up very, very high. — Would you like to?' Though posed as a question, how commanding it was! I would have liked to reply : 'Forgive me, not today.' It was already on the tip of my tongue, but some Satanic power put these words in my mouth instead : 'With the greatest pleasure.' Seeing that my will was paralysed, She made no more efforts to convince me, and we ascended almost without conversing. Oh, how dreadful were those hours! Like a dog I scurried behind Her; if She had thrown herself into the chasm, I would have thrown myself in after Her. We climbed higher and higher and were almost beneath the summit. She was becoming more and more nebulous and ghastly — finally I plucked up enough courage to manage : 'I have to turn back now' — yet at that very moment She anticipated me and said : 'Let's rest!' and I lay down next to Her like a lamb. She was now constantly biting her lips, and Her body seemed to be writhing in pain. After a while She walked behind the adjacent crag. I felt mortally weak like never before, more than was possible to explain by fatigue and agitation, yet even so my limbs felt lighter than ever before, as if they'd lost almost all their weight. Truly, some moments I couldn't even see my own body. Finally She appeared, cheery and carefree. 'Upwards! We'll be there soon!' — and Her lips pressed mine. We climbed up to the glacier miraculously quick. My limbs became lighter and lighter, and She helped me along. Shortly I felt as though lead were being poured into my veins . . . , and She was also becoming weaker, more sullen, until finally She said She would walk behind me. Her footsteps sounded odd, pattering softly, at times becoming almost inaudible, but for a long time I did not have the courage to turn round. Finally — — and horror! Her figure was flickering strangely, translucent like a column of water. I know for certain that I could see the crags through Her head. I sank to the ground, everything around was growing dark. And when everything started to brighten once more, She stood before me, laughing : 'What scared you so, madam?' I told Her. 'That's perfectly natural : everything flickers, disperses before the eyes, when one is about to faint — exhaustion, the thin, uncommon air at high altitudes — be so kind as to forgive me if I have caused you discomfort, you shall be richly recompensed.' She continued to laugh, while wiping away the blood running from her gnawed fingers and lips. 'For that matter, I am awfully nervous as well, and I've had a seizure, but I'm fine now. Upwards!' And with all the strength I had left I walked, She behind me. I felt as though some vampire were sucking the life out of me. The footsteps behind me began to fade again . . . Seized with a sudden dread I looked round — — and She was nowhere to be seen, even though I had heard Her just a few seconds before, even though that part of the mountain was entirely flat with no rocky outcrops, no hollows. Then, insane with fear,

I started running head over heels down the mountain. 'Off you go, off you go into the abyss that awaits you,' I heard behind me, all around me, but looking round again I did not see Her. Down, down! Then I heard your voice from the side, I recognised you. Naturally, in my terror I took you for another spectre in league with Her against me. Only much further down when I saw that neither you nor Her were in pursuit, when I had composed myself a little, I thought : 'Maybe he is Her victim, maybe She wanted to show me his death.' So I shouted at you to turn back, that your demise awaited you up there. But you did not hear me, or did not wish to. I'm glad she didn't wring your neck up there — and now it is your turn to tell me what happened to you!"

"I'll tell you later. Now tell me what has become of you since. Quickly, time is ticking away. Did you see Her after that?"

"A hundred times! Constantly. They call it hallucinating, but it is only the true vision of the truth. I am no longer able to distinguish Her from this table, or from you for instance; you saw that a moment ago — I thought you were a phantom. Only those who have experienced neither dreaming nor waking distinguish between the two — and dreaming is the same as vision and as death. These people here don't know this, and that is why I'm in a lunatic asylum. — She had lunch with me, washed with me from the same basin, tried on my dresses, She even polished my shoes once — and how many times has She slept by my side! But no one save myself has ever seen Her; so either I am mad or — everyone else is. I think it's them, even if there were a thousand jackasses here, they would make no more sense than a single one. Only you, you understand me! With you I will be of sound mind! The two of us will somehow make it work sensibly, even with Orea, won't we? We can even have a child together. We'll be all the happier for having been as unhappy as we've been till now. After all, beautiful weather eventually follows bad."

"Darling, the facts, quick!"

"All right then, calm down. I have not been to Stag's Head since. I've wanted to go. 'It would put an end to my suffering,' I told myself, but did not have the courage. What would have been the point of going there? I had Her here by my side all the time. So dreadfully close. Can you imagine it? Feeling boundless terror of Her, you tell yourself : 'No, I will no longer think about Her!' The terror slowly recedes — and then comes desire — 'to see Her just one more time and die' — you tell yourself — and you see Her again, and it's a wonder you do not die — and so it goes on and on in a vicious circle. I kept it a secret for a long time. Then I began to babble. My relatives — I am rich — hoped I would die. They brought in a psychiatrist to examine me. They bribed the villain, and he pretended to be a distant relative. If I had told him I was having hallucinations, they would have put me in some sanatorium for people with neurological disorders and nervous dispositions, but because I passionately advocated my conviction that Orea is a higher — more real — reality, I am here. Oh, the lunacy of humankind! But I don't condemn them, every little earthworm knows why it burrows into the soil —"

At that moment the door flew open, and a person wearing eyeglasses burst in, his eyes full of dumb rage.

"That's him, the psychiatrist, the villain they paid off!"

Errata cried out. "Darling Sider, protect me from him! Madness is hurtling towards me again — that — that — buttered bread roll —"

"You rogue, what are you doing here?" the professor screamed at Sider. "Which of the rascals here allowed you to — and you, you demented woman," he turned sharply towards Errata, grabbed her by the hair, and slapped her down into the chair. "That's your place, you animal!"

Though no heavyweight, Sider was athletic. He delivered the professor two slaps of such force that he slumped to the ground, his body twitching weakly. "I need to get out of here," flashed through Sider's mind. "I can't be arrested now. I need to put him out of action completely so he doesn't cause a commotion."

A lightning-quick blow to the temple — and the psychiatrist lay there like a corpse.

"Hurrah, hurrah!" Errata cried victoriously and started beating the man's face with her fists.

"My love," Sider pulled her away, "I must leave this place immediately. You are mine forever! Our destinies are inseparably bound! Together we will be victorious! Soon I will release you from here! In the meantime, let hope give you strength! I am with you always, do you hear? As for Her — that storm cloud will turn into an amorous, golden cloudlet! Bye!"

He gave her a last kiss and rushed out. "I am happy, my Sider, you will come, you will surely come, you will come soon, I believe it!" echoed behind him . . .

•

In his rapture Sider did not know quite what he was promising.

As he was fleeing the lunatic asylum he knew only one thing for certain : he must go away at once. Where to, he had no idea. He hopped on a train at random just as it was pulling out, having first purchased several of the most recent magazines and newspapers.

"Surely I will now read that Barbora was not murdered," he said to himself, having calmed down somewhat as the train set off. "In that case — back to Cortona!" But at that moment the horrific nature of Errata's account fully dawned on him . . . "I'm not going to have the strength to do it," he felt. "The hellishness of the whole affair might have tempted me before, now it only crushes me. I'm exhausted, I'm lost." He picked up a newspaper numbly and read :

"News of the murder of the oldest woman in our country, one-hundred-and-thirty-seven-year-old Barbora. On the basis of medical evidence, it has been ascertained beyond all doubt that the old woman was strangled. Among other indicators, strangulation marks were found on her neck. The iniquitous, clearly perverted perpetrator of this incredibly heinous crime has not yet been apprehended. Details of his appearance, however, are known (there followed a fairly accurate description of his person), as is the direction in which he fled. His probable destination is the town of N.N., known for its mental institution. The degenerate's motive was money, as indicated by the statement made

by Háta, the ninety-five-year-old daughter of Old Barbora, grief-stricken by the death of her dearly beloved mother, who said a sum of money went missing from the table drawer, as did some jewellery. Everyone hopes that this unprecedented scoundrel will end up in the hands of the penal system before long."

At the same time Sider chuckled a chill ran through his body that made him shudder, and this brought him relief. The heavy burden of having to make his own unprompted decision had fallen from his shoulders. — "Where to now?" he asked himself. "Ah, I will go home. The big city is the easiest place to get lost in. — And I have seen Her there on three occasions. I will go to Cliff Street : I feel Old Barbora's doppelgänger, a wise woman, will provide me with an explanation for all this. Yes, all my hopes lie with her at the moment . . . Damn it all, it's still not entirely certain that Orea is — the spirit of the mountain. Although Errata is not insane, she's about as far from being able to evaluate matters soberly as I am from having robbed Old Barbora's place. Yes, that's the way it is!"

He calmed down considerably. — He got off at the next station and, travelling by train, automobile, horse, foot, as circuitously as possible to put off his pursuers, he reached his hometown on 10 June.

He slept all morning and devoted the afternoon to disguising his appearance. Before leaving the house he instinctively took all the cash he had with him and took Orea's portrait out of the billfold he kept in his breast pocket. He looked at it for a long time and then placed it back in the billfold . . . Then he went to an out-of-the-way café, and there he read :

"New despicable crime committed by the murderer of Old Barbora. This pervert has apparently set his mind on paving his entire journey with the most nefarious crimes. On the fourth day of this month he broke into the mental institution in the town of N.N. There he cut the fetters that had been used to restrain insane patient Mrs E.S. so as to prevent her from committing suicide. No doubt he did so in order to be able to satiate his perverted lust with her. Upon being surprised by the most venerable scholar Professor N.N., he struck him several times in the head with a hammer and fled. A poor victim of his vocation, Professor N.N. was found unconscious by one of the orderlies. This man stated that he had been administered chloroform by the as yet unidentified scoundrel. In view of the fact that the man concerned is the thief from Old Barbora's place, there is no doubt that the fiend robbed the senseless scholar, even though he himself, having suffered nervous shock and only being able to react to everything by sobbing, cannot remember whether he had much money on him at the time. God willing, he will yet recall this fact. Mental patient Mrs E.S. places all the blame on herself, asserting that it was she who bludgeoned her kindly care provider with her fists. The absurdity of this assertion is self-evident. It is already known in what direction this hyena in human form fled from the institution. He is currently residing in the metropolis of N., and it is only a matter of hours before he is arrested."

Sider ran out of the café. At first he was totally beside himself. "Away, away from here, as far as possible, to the edge of the world!" was his only thought. "Somewhere into the inner provinces of China or the ancient forests of Ecuador . . . , as long as it is as far away as possible from all this horror so that it can finally end."

He jumped into a cab. After a moment he recalled that he was very near Cliff Street. A brief moment of indecision — "Ah, I'll go there one more time!" he decided. "Those few minutes won't kill me, should I leave Europe for good without being certain? I think not, I couldn't bear it, I would go mad abroad. I suspect that all will now be made clear."

·

The sun had just set when he reached the little black house. Dark clouds were rolling in from the south, a continuous bristle of lightning and ominous thunder. Sider hurriedly entered the hallway.

Once more he was standing before that familiar door. Will he again hear those eerie footsteps from afar, creeping along monstrously, madly, like the passing of time? No — instead he heard the shouting of children and a deep voice scolding them. He lit a match. "Daniel Škopek, Master Cobbler" — he read on the door. He knocked.

"Well, come in then!" the voice growled.

He entered. A kitchen modified into a cobbler's workshop. Four small children were rolling around on the floor; the shoemaker was sitting on his stool looking like he'd just drunk a quart of denatured spirits. A nagging woman's voice squawked from the adjoining room. "And yet the rooms are the same as they were in Cortona," he thought to himself as he said in confusion :

"Excuse me, is there an extremely old woman called Barbora living here?"

"What?" said the cobbler and stood up. "There's always only one woman here, and that's my wife, her name's Elisabeth, and even though the hag's already thirty-five, that doesn't make her extremely old just yet."

"About three weeks ago a hundred-year-old woman resided here, and a beautiful young lady was staying with her for a few days —"

"Holy Virgin, not again!" a woman's voice cried out, and the cobbler's missus burst into the kitchen, making the sign of the cross. The children started crying; the thunder roared so loudly that the little house shook. "I keep telling you, Škopek, this place is haunted!"

"Quiet, old bat! I've had just about enough of all this super-stitious nonsense! Keep your traps shut, you little brats!" and he raised his knee strap. "Esteemed sir, you seem like the brainy type, so please say if ye'd be serious, or if you've come to make a damn fool of me?"

"Has Old Barbora never lived here?" his legs were shaking so much that he sat down on the bench uninvited. "I quite certainly saw her here in the hall."

"The Lord above be with us," said the wife, "I also saw her! One evening when I was at home alone all of a sudden she shuf-fled through this kitchen so slowly it was just awful, and she went over there, to the bedroom! When I'd recovered enough to stand up again I ran after her and she wasn't there, and she couldn't have left because no door's there anymore and the windows were latched from the inside. Other people've seen her too, and sometimes also a handsome young gentleman and two pretty ladies, and the three of them dressed old-fashioned, like scarecrows, like the way they say people dressed during the time of Emperor Bonaparte. Husband, Škopek, I have no mind to live here a moment longer, I don't want to lose my marbles and customers don't want to come here."

"You old bat, go and peel the potatoes or I'll find another way to put your mind in order. What a load of rubbish! And here I thought we was living in an enlightened century. I'm no int'lect, just a workin' man, but a social democrat I've always been, and I don't believe nothin' — well, esteemed sir, ye'd best be on your way and close the door behind ye proper so we don't get struck by any lightnin' bolts God bungs our way —"

Sider stood in front of the house. All around torrents of rain cascaded down from a blackened sky, glowing sulfurously in the incessant infernal light of celestial flames. The voices of heaven roared like a hundred-strong pride of lions. But he did not hear them, did not see the lightning, did not feel the lashing of rain and hail . . .

"All is vanishing," thundered in his mind. "All is but a phantom . . . And still I have visible proof here!" Quickly he reached into his pocket, took out his billfold, leafed through it.

The portrait was not there. He looked through it again, thoroughly — nothing! "Yet I know, as certainly as I know that there was just a crash of thunder, that I placed it in one of the compartments before I left the house! She, too, has vanished, all reality has vanished, all reason, everything . . . — Away from here, from all of this — — where to, where to?"

Deliriously he fled into the insanely gleaming, insanely roaring, insane night — where to? Where to? . . .

5

He tramped round the globe. He lived in the high altitude regions of the Altai and the Cordillera, he lost himself in the wastelands of inner Australia, he walked across Africa. Not so much to elude the law as to flee from his ghastly love. The first he entirely succeeded in accomplishing, the second not at all . . . Like Errata, he still loved Orea, with horror, and he loved his horror and abhorred his loving, and it was driving him more and more mad. His eyes no longer beheld his beloved, and unlike Errata, he was not susceptible to "hallucinations," yet all the more profoundly did She lacerate his thoughts.

She had complete control of his thoughts, and all his efforts to rid himself of the appalling Lady were in vain. Distractions were futile. Futile were adventures, tiger hunting, intoxication by alcohol, opium, or other women. Futile was study, futile were the desperate efforts he made through stoicism, through viewing everything from a divine perspective. Nothing could banish the Ghost, his life's Destiny. His paradoxical life was but a vagary of Fate; he was not Its chosen one. Even when victorious, a mysterious torpidity would soon overcome him and straightaway he would rest on his laurels, each and every one. Never to be able to capitalise on one's victories is the most awful of fates. Everything has its time, and if that is frittered away, no use raising a corpse from the grave. A true, victorious force continues for years — through the whole of a life on its path to victory — that is the only way to conquer — the Struggle of Life. The day of Eternal Life, which was Sider's earthly life, had been predestined for something else.

Above all, he fought with Orea Herself. He reconciled himself to the idea that She was but a ghost, and he was even able to fall in love with Her as a ghost, — and he found it tremendously titillating. "To fear an apparition? What could be more nonsensical? — what could be more alluring, more seductive, than to love it, kiss it, share one's nights with it?" Her visits in his dreams were at times the most delightful his life had known. Sometimes he would rave in delight for a hundred days after one such night. He was filled with a peculiar subliminal pride that he loves, that he is loved by, a transcendental being. He felt the meaning of his life lay therein. But not all the joy in the world can gratify a person permanently, one merely becomes infatuated with it. A worm lives in order to suffer — : for the eternal Coming Joy, for the Storming the Walls of Heaven.

All of Sider's victories later led to a steadily advancing insanity

. . . As it was with Errata, whom he had promised to help and, needing help himself, was unable to, despite some rather feeble attempts . . . —

"Home! To where I used to see Her!" every part of his soul cried out in the end. "Come what may! Even if I'm executed, death is opening her jaws for me anyway. Let me go mad at once, let me burn in my madness, better than slowly rotting in it! Let the End roar, whatever is to happen, let it happen right now! I am — Her! Let me go up there, where She appeared to me, let me pursue my sacred, glorious Fate!"

This is what he told himself, and he obeyed, but only because of his irresistible compulsion, a fear of total disintegration, of helplessness, of being hemmed in — it was not the will, which spawns action. The state of his soul, the horror of the past years, were reflected in his face, which had become altered to such an extent it was almost unnecessary for him to use a disguise upon arriving in his hometown . . .

He arrived on the evening of 31 May, almost three years after having fled.

•

First thing the following morning, while it was still dawn, he was awoken by a furious pounding on the door of his room in the hotel where he had found temporary accommodation, not having had the courage to go to his own former apartment on the previous evening.

He opened. Errata stormed in. Her clothing was muddy and

in tatters, her haggard face grimaced wildly, Eternal Madness glared from her eyes as if they were windows.

"Salutations!" she guffawed loudly and spat in his eyes. "So, that was the one thing I still wished to do, you wretch, and now the devil can take me! I ran away from those curs in the madhouse, they're hard on my heels, but let them come and bark, I couldn't care less! You villain, you're worse than those scum! I placed all my hopes in you, but you didn't come to save me, you lied like a dog, I knew back then that you're a pathetic braggart, an impotent cripple, a measly phantom! Actually, you're de facto nothing but a miserable harpist whore, or a Debrecen sausage, I'm not quite sure which of the two just yet. You only came to me, you only slapped that dog around, to bring me even more misery. Oh, the beating they gave me after that! . . . At that point I truly did lose my mind; I'm still sane only to the extent that I know my sanity's gone. You were spineless in running away, as you run from everything, that's what I was told — by Her! But I have found you! Even though I didn't know where you were, I went with certainty, led by instinct, like a newly hatched turtle crawling unerringly towards an ocean it does not see, like a migratory bird finding its nest box from the previous year, like a cat taken miles away in a sack — I have found you, you anklebiter, how thin your calves are, yuck! Hee hee hee!"

"Sit down, Errata! Let me get you some decent clothing," he was hardly able to string a few words together, and he placed his hand on her nape.

"Don't touch me, you harpist!" she shrieked and punched him in the face. "You, you are the cause of my ruin and — Hers!

Just so you know : back in the loony bin I told you the most exquisite lies, not a word of it true, hee hee! I had told myself : the best thing would be if I punish the scoundrel by tricking him into thinking Orea is a ghost. And he, the lunatic, really believed it! Now my best revenge will be to tell you the truth : She is a real female creature just like myself! I had known Her for years before I met you in Cortona, you dunce. She was a wealthy lady who stayed every year in a summerhouse on the other side of Stag's Head. As we're both a bit eccentric, we became friends, and we made an agreement that we would frighten superstitious fools to amuse ourselves. We cared for each other. But when a male scumbag like you gets in the way, female friendship is over. That evening in the ravine we made a pact to make you lose your marbles, seeing as you really didn't have any. Then on that Sunday we, stupid ninnies, both fell hard for you and became jealous of each other, like cats. You twit, She didn't vanish from me up there, we just had a catfight because of you, you wretch. She was bleeding from the lip because I had punched Her. 'You can gobble him up for all I care, bon appétit!' I told Her when I'd tousled Her hairdo, and then I ran down. 'Let him have his way with Her up there, the slut,' I said to myself, 'so he can see what shrivelled breasts she has.' I ran past you on purpose, as if I didn't see you — and only once I got to the bottom did I holler : 'A fine whore you're clambering after!' I later lost my mind only because I loved you just a wee bit and couldn't find you — everything is becoming muddled — She kept crawling after me, but it wasn't a hallucination, just lesbianism —"

Exhausted, she slumped into a chair. "My dear Errata, you

know what? Put on one of my suits, that will be the most sensible thing to do, that way they won't recognise you, and then let's leave this town! This time I will save you —"

Her eyes closed, she did not answer for some time. Then she reached between her breasts and pulled out a piece of chalk. "Look," she laughed triumphantly, "I found this for you! On the street, of all places! Things like this are rolling around outside!" and she started to draw something resembling an animal on the door. Suddenly she jerked violently. "Hah, do you hear that? They're coming after me already, those curs! Do you hear them barking? They're coming, they're coming, it's the end, the end of everything!"

"My dear Errata, that's just the milkman's dog barking outside."

"No, it's them! I know today is the day of deliverance! When I was lying in the forest last night, She appeared to me and said : 'Tomorrow you will be with me, freed forever from the human madhouse.' Orea, my beloved, I am coming to You, to You!" and quick as lightning she deftly seized an unsheathed dagger that Sider had placed on his bedside table in case the police arrived. "I cannot fall into their hands again, I swore to that! Get away, you scoundrel!"

She leapt swiftly to the wall and in a flash plunged the steel twice into her heart . . . — "Orea, my love, my sister, I see You, You are smiling at me, I am Yours, Your arms open for me, I am Yours in Eternal Radiance, and yours, too, my Sider!"

Those were the last words of sweet, revered Errata, the last words in this most delusive world we call "the waking state," "reality," beyond which the light of lights thunders — yet only for those who have at least beheld its glimmer — — —

Sider thought it most sensible if he himself performed the last service for his lover. Having dwelled for a moment, shedding a few tears over the body as it grew cold, he left resolutely for his house. The hour was propitious, the streets still virtually deserted. Having keys both to the main door of the building and to his apartment allowed him easy entry. Although the fact that many objects had been moved gave evidence that the authorities had been there, he found his rooms in more or less the same state as he had left them. Taking some things with him, including a large suitcase and several books, he hurried back to the hotel. Nothing suggested that Errata's arrival and death had been observed. Her body was terribly withered and light as a feather. He packed it into the suitcase, and that very morning he took her to a place just outside of town which he had already selected many years before in case he would have to deal with any delicate situations . . . an easily overlooked section of a rocky valley. Standing atop its modest slopes it was possible to see a kilometre in the distance all around to make sure no one was approaching. In one particular spot, a vertical wall of weathered slate, heavily eroded underneath, rose above the bottom of the small valley. Sider placed his precious cargo beneath it — several prods with his walking stick — and three cubic metres of rock crashed down onto the suitcase. The entire procedure took less than a minute. Sweet Errata was buried deeper than in a normal grave.

Errata lies not in a loathsome cemetery common to members of the vile, rabid humanity that tortured her to death : the former casing of Her eternal Soul dissolves into atoms far from them, in a peaceful, clean nook rarely ever defiled by human foot — but like the soul, the casing, too, is immortal; in the maternal embrace of its immense tumulus-monument, the everlasting, darkly dreaming rocks, it also dreams here darkly, quietly, monotonously, sweetly and for endless time . . . Her redeemed, liberated Spirit shines more radiantly than the sun, graciously warming the cliff and Errata's dust from above; more swiftly than the ether it flies, scintillating and thundering. —

Over the next few days he lingered in town, not visiting his apartment, spending every night in a different hotel, or sleeping out in the open. For the time being he was not pestered by the police. Every evening he wandered through the streets, hoping to see Orea once more.

Despite the grisly incident with Errata, his state of mind somewhat improved. For the first time in three years Sider's mind entertained the hope that Orea might just be a human being after all. It was a faint hope, frail, nourished more by desire than probability. — Yet it became considerably stronger when on 6 June he read the following in one of the Alpine magazines :

"Finally! The person who, having exploited the superstition prevalent in the environs of Stag's Head, has been frightening gullible persons by impersonating the ghost of this mountain was apprehended on the 20th of May of this year. She is a lady still in her younger years, beautiful and exceptionally well educated. For a number of years her lodging has been a summerhouse in the hamlet of N. at the foot of Stag's Head. She has not yet divulged what motivated her to cultivate this surely rather peculiar sport,

especially for a lady as distinguished as she. According to the conclusions of experts, she likely displays special abilities of animal magnetism, hypnotism, and telepathy. More light will be cast on this case as the investigation continues."

The first idea that occurred to the now exhilarated Sider was to set off to the mountains and liberate his love from prison. But because the arrest had taken place seventeen days ago, he concluded that it would do no harm to first find out what had happened in the meanwhile to the incarcerated woman. His fervour cooled even more when he considered the strangling of Old Barbora . . . He got hold of as many newspapers as possible from Alpine countries, even writing to their editors, as well as to the courthouse where the lady was being held. His mood considerably brightened.

But a new, significant event raised his hopes enormously. It was not until 9 June that he opened one of the books he'd taken with him from his apartment on that dreadful morning, and tucked away in it he saw — Orea's portrait with Her handwritten note! . . . He was so dumbfounded that it fell from his hand.

"A miracle, or did I in a moment of incomprehensible distraction insert it in the book myself? I could swear now as then that I put it in my billfold . . . But what do I know? What does anyone know with absolute certainty? Can you ever be entirely sure if you're rowing a boat or skating on ice, if you're not at that exact moment the victim of a mysterious veiling of the senses and the soul? Of a delusion, a vision, somnambulism? If awake or dreaming? There is nothing, nothing you can swear by; we will never know anything with certainty as long as the spirit is the spirit, i.e., Illusion . . ."

He had Orea once again! How tremendous! A thousand times a day he took the portrait from its sleeve to check that it had not vanished. A little monkey does not look at the shard of a mirror as often as he at the spectral, intoxicating visage and the magical handwriting. His hope in Orea's reality transformed into an absolute, almost blissful belief, for he did not want to doubt — he could not permit himself to doubt . . . He saw his only salvation herein. He naturally could not destroy his scepticism, though he did manage to narcotize it and subjugate it to his faith. Greatly invigorated and restored to health, he was able to feel in the same way as a long time before : "And if in the most extreme case She were a ghost, that too would be beautiful!" His soul, timorously hesitant, having suffered serious injury, crippled, had yet to rally in full. Otherwise he would have set off at once for Cortona without a second thought. It should be said that what was holding him back more than the dread of making a final decision was the fear of ending up behind bars. Wavering pathologically, he regretted his inability to come to a decision.

•

Though no reports about the fate of the arrested woman reached him, he did read in one magazine this paragraph dated 14 June :

"*The tragedy of a mother and daughter.* On the ninth of this month around midnight an enormous rock crashed down on an old, dilapidated cottage in Cortona. The rock, which as if by a miracle had hung above the house since beyond human memory, demolished it completely. Its only inhabitant, a ninety-eight-year-old woman commonly known as Barbora's Háta, was found in the rubble mortally wounded. She gave up the ghost a few hours later after receiving the grace of holy confession and last rites. We note that the mother of the deceased, one-hundred-and-thirty-seven-year-old Barbora, encountered a similarly tragic death in the same dwelling three years ago, having been strangled to death by a villainous robber who thus far has unfortunately eluded arrest." —

On the morning of the following day, 15 June, he walked boldly into Cliff Street. The sun was shining from an unblemished sky. —

The black house was in ruins. Workers were knocking down the remains of the walls, between which the wife of Master Cobbler Daniel Škopek was crawling around in the rubble on her knees with her two children.

Sider sat down on a nearby lawn for a moment. Then he walked up to the woman :

"What happened, dear lady?"

She stood up, shielding her eyes with the palm of her hand, and half-slumped down onto the rubble, half-embraced Sider's knees. "Noble sir, handsome young gentleman, you came to warn us before, the last time, but we didn't heed your warning! Actually, not so much me, Škopek was the one who wouldn't listen — the Lord be merciful to his soul," she started crying, "he's with the Lord's truth now."

"What happened?" he repeated frostily.

"Why the house fell down, didn't it, noble sir!"

"What day was that?"

"Please hold on a second . . . It was — Sunday last —"

"So the ninth. How did it happen?"

"Noble sir, I'll gladly tell ye everything — don't gawp, you brats, keep looking! — a few packets of hobnails must still be lying around here somewhere, dear sir, we need every heller."

He gave her a large banknote. "No need for that," he pushed away her lips from his hand. "Tell me what happened!"

"On that fateful night no earthly power could get me to fall asleep. Then I remembered that I had laundry up in the attic, and because it was raining and the roof was full of holes I went to fetch it. It was around half eleven. So as I'm walking down the hallway on the upper floor, I see there's a strip of light beneath the door to the room — for the love of God! I open the door — and noble sir, my legs still buckle beneath me — two beautiful ladies and a handsome young man were sitting there by the table, all of them dressed like scarecrows, in old clothes, like Emperor Bonaparte. And then one of the ladies, she was wearing a blue dress, raised her glass, and there was thick frothy blood in it. She clinked glasses with the other two, who also had blood in their glasses, and said — Mother of Jesus, I almost fainted when I heard that voice of hers :

" 'A great night it is tonight, even greater is the Day to come, here's to all-reconciling Death! Here's to Eternal Redemption! Here's to glorious Nemesis!'

"The other lady whooped and clinked her glass, and the gentleman hesitated a bit, and then he clinked his glass too. And they all drank the thick blood.

"I don't know how I survived it. And then I was suddenly scarpering down the stairs. 'Škopek!' I shouted, 'there's ghosts upstairs! Put your trousers on quick,' I told him, 'and get up there!'

"He grumbled, but in the end he went up. In the meantime I was praying, and my teeth were chattering. He came down and said : 'Crazy bitch, there's nothing up there, why did you wake me, you sow!' and he thrashed me with his knee strap, but I didn't even feel it, such was the horror still rattling me. As soon as he'd finished beating me he lay back down and fell asleep, snoring. I dropped to my knees and started to pray. Then the tower struck midnight and all of a sudden — it was like an enormous stone fist struck the roof . . . — and our ceiling caved in, and one of the beams fell on that heathen — the Lord God forgive me — right on his head. His brain squirted out," she started weeping. "He was a social democrat and a fool, but may the Lord grant him eternal glory!"

"How could the roof have collapsed?"

"That I don't know, gracious sir. The master builder, he's over there, go ask him if it be to your liking, said he doesn't understand it, said the beams were in fine shape, that it looks just like a rock had fallen on the roof. Go ask him yourself, kind sir!"

"There's no need any longer . . . Is there anything else you can tell me?"

"Well, only that I came to no injury, blessed be the Lord, my children neither. But, dear, noble sir, how shall a widow such as I provide for four hungry mouths? Oh dear God —"

Sider gave her a fistful of banknotes of sufficient value to allow her and her children to live without care for several years, and then he quickly departed.

She caught up with him and, falling to her knees, clasped his waist :

"Dear sir, what have you, for the sake of Christ, given me! Why, it's an entire fortune."

"Forgive me it's so little. *I* am the one who demolished the house."

"Most honourable sir — what — aaah! — You do resemble that gentleman who drank the blood — you're like two peas in a pod you are — aaah . . . take your money —"

"What good is it to *me*, ha ha ha ha!" he laughed and hurried away. "Madman, cretin!" the yelling of the boys hounded him. —

"Is She human? . . . But what is a human? Ha ha ha! Is She a ghost? . . . Am I not a ghost? Ha ha ha! I do not know anything about anything. Everything human falls; I am falling; what a joy it is to fall; the human's fall is God's liberation . . . To the Alps! . . . But I feel so enervated right now, so savagely, so helplessly weak — thrice weak! . . . My demise is imminent, that much is certain . . . Oh heavens above or Will of mine, give me the strength not to end up in a dunghill, but in Radiance! . . . Sleep . . . ; or a bullet to the head right away? How repulsive the will! . . ."

He found himself wandering the streets around midnight. He had no idea how he came to be standing in Cliff Street. "It's no use!" he laughed lethargically. "Ah, ah, the light of the full moon at solstice is completely yellow, sickly, and something is whispering to me . . . Let's go there, there — there we will sleep, there the pistol, there the bullet . . ."

He walked into the rubble. He wound his way through piles of stones and bricks. Among them, he noticed something blue, quivering, the appearance of a human body. He came nearer, cold as death. It was a woman, lying on her side, her face covered with her palms and a kerchief.

"It's Her," he said to himself, "of course, who else? Real or a phantom? Do I have the portrait?" he reached into his pocket, and at once withdrew his hand. "Ridiculous questions, to hell with it all! She is, therefore She is not, She is not, therefore She is! Ah!"

He lay down next to Her and looked at Her. He was in a strange state of mind, not afraid and yet lacking the courage to address Her . . . "What is it that the moon keeps whispering to me? It's something important but I still don't understand . . . Aaah — what was that? It felt as though my entire soul had turned 360 degrees . . . But how light, free, brave I feel —"

He reached out swiftly to tear the kerchief from the woman's face. He was struck by such a strong jolt of electricity he remained momentarily transfixed.

"Orea," he said softly after a while.

Silence.

"Say something to me at last!"

Silence.

"I love You, I'm unhappy, help me!"

Silence. But Her shoulders twitched ever more vigorously.

"Do You not hear me, my most beloved?"

— — "I am not allowed to speak," She said after a moment in a whisper as hollow as a puff of wind.

"And yet You've spoken."

"I should not have — —"

"What am I to do? Have mercy!"

A moment of silence. "Liberate me . . ." thundered after a longer while.

"Free me first . . . I'm weak and sickly. I do not have the courage — for Cortona."

"You must!"

"I cannot."

Feverishly She shook, and then all of a sudden —

"Very well then, I shall give you your wish! I will be punished severely for it, as will you. Nothing in eternity has more deplorable consequences than making things easier for oneself : whoever makes things easier, makes things worse, whoever helps, harms. We, however, can bear it. So — here is my kiss!"

She threw off the kerchief. And he beheld Her terribly beautiful, beautifully terrible face, whiter and more lustrous than the moon above. Her arms embraced him — "My eternal Sider" — and Her lips touched his. A horrible moment, he felt as though someone were ripping his soul from his body, like pulling a tooth. Then the blackness of terror burst into the radiant flames of unbounded delight . . . he saw Her recoil and Her snow-white hands shield Her face from his — but once again and more vehemently She lunged into his embrace. Everything then became immersed in darkness.

When Sider regained consciousness the east was quietly,

spectrally turning white, the moon turning vitreous. He suddenly felt himself to be a *completely* different person than he had ever been before : steadfast and strong, heroic, noble. He rose. Only then did he see the woman lying a step away.

She was wearing a blue dress, its appearance indicating a filthy whore. Bared breasts, knees uncovered, an ordinary face. Snoring appallingly, the stench of liquor issuing from her gaping mouth reached all the way to his nostrils . . .

"Ha ha! So this apish world we inhabit behaves consistently! Of no consequence, entirely insignificant. Nothing that humans know has anything to do with the depth of Primordial Existence. Humankind only floats on a surface of mud; it is itself mud. Out from the mud! . . . Oh, how everything, everything that a moment ago was crushing me seems so ridiculously light now! Thanks to You, Orea! Soon I will be Yours, holy goddess, soon I will be — God! . . . My Orea, how trivial the question if You are human or phantom! Whether one or the other, for me both now are one and the same! — I'm coming to You — to Eternity!" —

He walked directly to the railway station, bright and powerful like the rising sun.

6

He arrived in Cortona on the afternoon of 17 June.
The clean, unblemished sky hung above him radiantly like
an immense blue sun in which our own ostensible sun drowns
like the paltry human being in God. The awful ranks of the
mountains of Cortona — fossils of the primeval Melody thundering : "Do what you can, worm, and don't worry about the
rest, you will be squashed no matter what, just a slightly bigger
germ you are! Though this you fail to understand."

That is how they spoke to him, and he, a wretched human,
did understand a little : at least he understood that he did not
understand — yet under all circumstances this is what is most
important down here. Is it good to understand anything? Is it
even possible? . . . For the human, understanding means madness and death. And Sider no longer wished to understand, and
with his soul ablaze he strode into his dear, ghastly little town.

His inner being experienced no ordinary human joy, let alone merriment. Pain and Horror ruled, but they were of a kind that embraces all the joy and light of the world in a glorious, weighty reconciliation. Lofty melodies marched through his soul majestically like columns of long dead, spectral armies — funeral processions that are the Dithyramb of Rebirth. —

He spent the afternoon in the hotel, writing in rapt delight, trying to cram into a few pages his entire life and soul — his last testament. In the evening, he went to the garden restaurant, and he sat in a dark corner, blissfully drinking his wine, content. The warm fragrant evening nestled up to him as if to implore : "Do not abandon earthly seductiveness!" He laughed at it, knowing that Tomorrow will again be a Day, that Tomorrows and Mornings will be eternal.

He had altered his appearance as best he could, though not from fear : "If they arrest me, I will not be able to free Her . . ."

Suddenly a colossal figure waddled towards him. "Oh, the local doctor!" he said to himself and slightly averted his face. Even so, the figure stopped in front of him. It was clear the dear doctor was once again in a buoyant mood, if not yet inebriated.

"Hey, don't we know each other?"

"We do," Sider said and laughed.

"Hell, you've disguised yourself! You can't fool me. I'd recognise your eyes even if under ten pairs of green glasses. — Hah, you're Old Barbora's murderer!" he bellowed so loudly the other guests sitting nearby started to get up. "I've finally caught you! Hey, police, over here!"

Sider calmly removed his glasses. "Forgive me, Orea, that we won't see each other tomorrow on the mountain. Forgive me all this social dirt. *I* am guilty of it. Forgive me for being a human . . . ," and smiling he looked at the doctor.

"Well look here, he's not afraid!" the doctor said in disappointment, having scrutinised Sider's face for a while. "Aha, you already know what old lady Háta confessed to!"

"I do not."

"Hey," the doctor boomed, sitting down slowly next to Sider, "how much longer is it going to take, headwaiter, footwaiter?"

"Here you go, kind sir!" said the waiter, bringing the usual bottle of cognac.

The doctor drank a quarter litre in one go. "Ah, ah —," he let off some steam while stroking his belly. "A man can't even wet his lips while hard at work all day." He turned to Sider : "I have to admit that I behaved towards you — a bit inhumanly — yes, like a pig . . . But I knew that you already knew about Háta's confession."

"That Old Barbora wasn't strangled —?"

"Nonsense, man! Háta was the one who strangled her. Yes, yes, don't look at me like that! 'That gentleman,' she said, 'is as innocent as a lily. As he was running away my mother started to come round, and I, now filled with joy that the Lord had finally called her to Him, couldn't stand it anymore and committed sin.' "

"So why did she strangle her?" Sider asked nonchalantly.

"My dear little friend, now that you've turned yourself into a psychologist, it's rather interesting for you. She confessed to strangling her mum not because she had been a burden to her,

Háta, for so long, and it wasn't out of mercy either, from not being able to bear the sight of someone perpetually half-dead, not even because she imagined she'd actually be doing a good deed, nor on account of any inheritance — after all, for thirty-five years she had been de facto owner of the house and all belonging to it. No : this was about formal ownership, the legal title. She said she had dreamed for years of seeing in black and white on the official deed : Háta, owner of cottage number such and such."

"A very good illustration," Sider remarked, "of the inconceivable perversity of human nature. To not shrink from murdering one's own mother and incriminating an innocent person for the most despicable crime because of something so trivial. It's an interesting twist of Fate that she died in the rubble of her own shack."

"Ha ha, you, my dear fellow, are as superstitious as the God-fearing people of these parts! — Well, no need to fear anything any longer you brigand, and let's raise our glasses to that!" He poured another glassful down his gullet. "Ah, ah —"

"I've also been charged with an offence I actually committed, an act of violence against your dear friend the psychiatrist."

"Nonsense! Our state does not extradite foreign nationals for some lousy fiddle-faddle like knocking someone unconscious. Even if it turned out not to be the case, it would just be a fine of a hundred or so, now that you're known to be neither a murderer nor a thief — and he's a cretin and a scoundrel! Don't you dare doubt that, or you'll have me to contend with! After all, you're the one responsible for giving his gob such a fine smacking! You'd never done anything worthwhile in your life, but for sorting him out like this the Lord will forgive you all your misdeeds. Damn it, you're my friend, you went there just to avenge me! I'm supposed to have dementia praecox — the rogue!" He stood up and waved his arms as though fencing with an invisible adversary. "I wonder if you know, my dear fellow, that this payback has turned him, merely a nitwit before, into a complete imbecile? He's suffered a softening of the brain since; he has dementia praecox. He no longer even knows the difference between a vein and an artery, and he can't tell the difference between convex and concave glass; recently he ordered convex glasses for one farsighted lunatic, ha ha! And the swine has started drinking to boot, and he's bringing the entire medical profession into disrepute with his constant drunkenness. I'm surprised they haven't thrown the rascal out yet."

"But have you, Doctor, been bestowed the recognition and honours you undoubtedly deserve over these past three years?"

"Of course I have, my dear fellow. I was appointed medical councillor and awarded the Order of St. George First Degree."

"Do you know anything about Mrs Errata S. escaping from the lunatic asylum?"

"You little rascal, how could I not know, I of all people!?"

"I'm not suspected of her murder, am I?"

"Listen, you don't suffer from persecution mania, do you? They couldn't care less about you. They found her in the pond right behind the asylum — she'd hung herself, or more accurately, she'd drowned."

"Did they prove her identity beyond any doubt?"

"Absolutely. You really are a moron."

"And who was the lady arrested a month ago allegedly for scaring people on Stag's Head?"

"I'll tell you that as well. She's the wife of an industrialist who tramped over to the other side of the mountain for a summer vacation for the first time this year. Young, dishy, she has three children and a head full of straw; nothing eccentric about her. The devil only knows why she twice tried to scare people on the mountain, and really stupidly at that. She hung green brushwood on her body from head to toe and howled at people up on the slopes. They caught her soon enough. At first she claimed she was the one who had been frightening people out of their wits up there for so many years, but once she had been shown that this was impossible, she broke down in tears and admitted that the real spirit of Stag's Head appeared to her once in the forest and ordered her, so she said, to haunt the place in her stead during May. She claimed she was to serve as bait that some unknown person would run after. She had completely succumbed to the power of this suggestion, spoke under its influence even while in detention. Even so, she was set free."

Only a slight shudder ran through Sider upon hearing this news, which a few days before would have totally crushed him, as it meant the death sentence for him. "What's your view on the whole matter?" he inquired coldly.

"Someone was responsible for those pranks, of course. It stands to reason it wasn't a ghost. Or are you, my dear friend, such a noodlehead to believe it was? You know what it was? It was a man dressed up as a woman! A strong, nimble, cunning rascal, just like yourself. He also had the power of animal magnetism, hypnotic abilities — tele– telepathic, you pathetic lump. He also understood science. Do you know what science is, you rummy?" This word reminded him of the duties of a guest and he downed another glass. "Ah, ah! . . . hocus pocus it was, pres–ti–digitation, electricity and trick photography," he said with a mighty hiccup that sounded like a dog barking, "all in all a load of humbug like that silly novel *The Castle of the Carpathians.* In the story some prima donna walks along the castle batt–le–ments — and she sings — but she's been long dead, just as dead as you're a complete pig — and don't you get it? all of it was science! Do you know what science is? Science is — science," he roared like a bull, "and anyone who doesn't believe in science hook, line, and sinker has me to answer to — you crackpot, you — superstitious — ninny —"

He reached for his glass again, which the waiter had refilled in the meantime, but he knocked it over. Without even noticing, he drank from the empty glass. "Ah, ah! . . ." And suddenly becoming tender : "I told you off, but I respect you, I adore you, you swine — but mark the words of a wise, sixty-year-old man — don't take stock in sup– super– superstition — be po– po– positive — I behave like a pig sometimes, but I always know what I'm say– saying. I — I'm a good person — and that cretin the psychiatrist alleges I have dementia pr– pr. Psychiatrist — nonsense — that's no science! There's no soul, only matter — the brain — there's no psycheee, so therefore there's no psychiatrist either, especially not one that's such a scoundrel, who drinks like a fish every day, attends to his patients drunk, or topples over even before he gets to see them — and someone like that tells me that I have dem–, my dear sir, something like that hurts, until the end of my days it will gnaw at my heart." His head fell onto his elbows and he started to weep loudly.

"It was a pleasure, Doctor," Sider squeezed his shoulder and started walking away.

"Stop, stop, traitor!" the doctor roared and stood up. Sider walked on. "Stop! I loved you affectionately, stop!"

Sider turned round. The doctor rushed towards him like a rhinoceros charging at full tilt. Sider stepped out of the way, and the doctor would have taken a dive had Sider not caught him and sat him down on the nearest bench with a quick jerk. But the physician showed no appreciation for this good deed, and having recovered, he brayed :

"Ha ha! Now I recognise you, You're the psychiatrist! You and no one else! That noble gentleman who slapped you around, he's my greatest friend! Don't deny it, villain! You killed all your patients — ha ha, only now I know — you, you are the ghost of Stag's Head — don't deny it, scumbag, you're that charlatan of science, you're that — Castle of the Carpathians," — he fell back on the bench and mumbled — "I — I — po– po– positivism —"

As he was leaving, Sider could hear the sound of heavy snoring.

•

The tops of the western mountains glittered with gold under the gaze of the rising sun as Sider rose from his bed after the most beautiful of all sleeps : the kind that when waking seems like a second and eternity simultaneously, having been a single triumphant stream of infinite, adamantine, otherworldly, and yet entirely *forgotten* dreams. — He went to the window and opened it.

He had never seen a sky so stupefyingly, vertiginously blue and deep, never had he heard birdsong so polyphonic and sparkling, never before had such powerful currents of such mystical fragrances rushed towards him. For a long, long, long time he stood there in celestial ecstasy. And as the invisible sun, incandescent gold sublimated into gas, rose higher and higher, lower and lower its powerful, golden gaze descended down the sides of the western colossi, just as the more a thought rises towards God, the more it descends into the lowlands and the swamps of humanity . . . The golden robe had already slid down from the crown of Stag's Head almost to its foot when for the second time — now standing — Sider awoke from a dream.

"How beautiful it is *here,* as if Earth had gathered all her jewels into one pile and thrown them before me, beseeching : 'Don't leave me!' And to be honest — I'm almost tempted — — perish the thought, you're not allowed even to knock on my door today! See, your finger just grazes my door — and already I'm somehow atremble . . . Away with you, ogre, for I am going to my execution — ugh, ugh, this thought will continue to menace me if I don't snuff it out while it's still embryonic! . . . Love of the earth is the mother of all cowardice, its only mother; courageous is every thought of Eternity; to see *sub specie aeternitatis* — and Courage itself — these are identical concepts to the core! . . ."

He quickly added a few lines to the pages he'd written the

day before, looked at photographs of his parents and a few of his other most cherished items — and abruptly he cast everything aside in irritation and quickly got dressed. His sublime mood returned in full.

He was ready; once more he went to the window. "I was in this very room on that hauntingly beautiful morning when, as I was about to leave, I saw the coloured dots up there on the mountain . . . That day was just as blue and just as bewitching . . . Today I am also leaving — though I'm going a bit further . . . But — am I mistaken? Nothing — might happen up there. Maybe in the end it will all turn out to have been a dreary farce — as is customary in this world of ours. Will I see — Her today of all days? . . . It's a paradox — but no, I feel that my soul will *evoke* Her, *must* evoke Her! She has turned into an enchanted orchard whose irresistible allure attracts all the magical birds of the cosmos. There is not the slightest atomic quiver that has not been caused solely, solely by —Will; only those who lack it seek causes elsewhere, in something outside of themselves, in 'nature,' in 'God' . . . Farewell, little room, to a speedy Reencounter!"

Turning away from the window something suddenly startled him. He looked — and slowly turned pale . . .

On the side of Stag's Head, about 100 metres above Cortona, he saw two dots : blue and — — — red . . . He grabbed his field glasses. Yes, they were ascending, very slowly . . . ; without a doubt it was the women . . .

"Just like before . . . ! Sublime horror of the All — how lethally my soul is being flooded by — an otherworldly Niagara . . . Orea! Also — — Errata! Graves are opening. Eternity herself is flinging her arms around me — I must not sink —

"But is it Errata? . . . Right now it's nothing more than a red dot. I'm being ridiculous by jumping to conclusions . . . Maybe even Orea — . . . Maybe yesterday that doctor fellow was right after all. It's not out of the question that it's all some infernal, fiendish hocus-pocus. Strictly speaking, everything, everything, even what happened in Cliff Street, could always be explained in 'a completely natural way,' whether it's supernatural phenomena sanctioned by science, such as 'suggestion,' 'telepathy,' or 'hallucination,' — and of course by timeless design, finality in All-Happening — which of course thus becomes God . . . Pah to all these imbecilic human concepts! The concept of reality is nonsensical — it was only created by beggarly animalistic conceit — as was its complement : illusion! — no : fantastic Super-Splendour is the All! : and therein lies the alpha and omega of wisdom! Enough! Orea — Errata — I am coming, coming to you! I will behold the Sun itself where before I saw only the reflections of its reflections . . ."

The sun's first sparkle burst above the mountain as Sider walked out to the street.

"I would like to have a look at what remains of Barbora's house . . . Should I — or no? Ah, those dots won't run away from me, and running away, they'd want me to catch up with them, just like all women do. Might something important still await me there?"

He stood in front of a pile of rubble and crushed rocks. Evidently the site had remained undisturbed, as if everyone had been afraid to touch the ruins . . .

For a while he waded through the rubble, climbed up onto the pile . . .

"Nothing out of the ordinary," he said to himself, "except over there — probably the blood of sweet Háta . . ." He was climbing back down when he saw a box rusted through and through sticking out of the remains of one of the walls. He had no trouble pulling it out as it had apparently been hidden in a secret cache in what had formerly been the wall. He cracked it open easily with a stone, and he discovered a thick journal.

The handwriting had faded and was mostly illegible, likely written by a woman's hand. The language, clearly Romanic, was almost incomprehensible to Sider. Judging by the frequent dates at the beginnings of paragraphs, it was a diary.

But what was it that sent shivers through Sider as he viewed the handwriting? Yes, it was identical to the handwriting on the back of the Portrait . . . He leafed through it and saw an ink drawing — a woman's face — Her — face . . . In a mystical way he felt as though he had drawn it himself a long time ago. And more than once he distinctly read : "Orea" . . .

The last date was 18 June 1820. Not a single word followed — —

"Today is also 18 June, and the year — 1920," he shuddered . . . "18 June — ah, I remember : the day the ancient Greeks consecrated to Nemesis . . . I read in a work by a certain historian : 'It is the day when two of the greatest military leaders of the new era felt the claws of Fortune — august Hohenzollern at Kolín, illustrious Bonaparte at Waterloo.' And I — — — So — after all? . . . How gruesome!"

And now for the first time true fear, bordering on horror, shot through him. "Did I *in the depths of my soul* still hope it would not come to pass? Was it merely a delusion that I actually wished it would happen?"

Unwittingly he looked up at Stag's Head, darkly hoping he would not see the dreadful dots again. He saw them once more, a little higher . . .

"Shameful thoughts be gone!" he called out, and tossed aside the journal and hurried away from the place as quickly as he could, employing all his strength to regain his former sublime mood. He succeeded. "But," he still felt, "grim battles surely await me up there! Yet — so be it! all the better for it! Shameful it is to wish to achieve anything great on the cheap, without the sublime final Victory."

He walked through the garden of the restaurant, quickly made his way up through the forest. He found himself in a clearing. A cottage stood there. A debt collector was just leading a cow through the gate, a young woman surrounded by children was kissing its muzzle, wetting it with her tears.

"What does the debt come to?" — He paid it and gave the woman everything he had down to the last heller; it still amounted to several thousand ducats. He ran upwards so fast the woman receiving his gift could only reach him with her cries —

"May the Lord endow the kind gentleman with another hundred years of life —"

"Perhaps I did this to demolish even this tiny financial bridge behind me! . . . No. If everything in the end does turn out to be a farce, nothing's easier than managing to get out of here some-how, and once home, because I'm no longer viewed by people as a villain, I have enough real estate assets . . . No, I do not want 'life,' I want Eternity. One hundred years of life she wished me, ha ha! How modest people are! If I cannot have Eternity, I don't want anything!" —

He came out of the forest onto rocky ground. And again he saw at a great height above him the monstrous dots, now con-siderably larger, just like before. For the first time he rested, but there was no need : the majesty of the soul gives the body wings; woe to today's airplane obsessed, crutch-reliant humanity that does not understand this.

He climbed higher and higher. The dots drew nearer — vanished — then appeared again, — in exactly the same way as before. "Have I fallen through time to fifteen years ago? I read a fairy tale like that once, what is this reality? . . . I am really curious if the one in red will come charging down again."

Once again he saw them resting not far from the glacier. He also rested. Then all three once more began their ascent.

Everything down in the valley was becoming smaller and punier. Cortona transformed into several crisscrossing lines as if drawn by a stick in sand. Along with his body — Sider's spirit rose higher and higher above the ground. He felt he was the Sublime itself and Eternal Enchantment, as though the other-world — the World-Miracle, to which he was drawing near, as he was to the sun, was already irradiating his soul with its thunder-ing refulgences.

At the fork he turned left. He was glancing to the side all

the time now, in case he saw the scarpering woman . . . Then he heard steps directly above him — charging right at him — — Errata.

He was only slightly startled. She was already standing before him, young and beautiful, just like then — she, who was decomposing far away in the burial mound beneath the cliff in a small coffin of leather . . . And — she fell into his arms and — kissed him . . .

Yet it was as if all his strength had been sapped all at once . . .

She withdrew. "Go, dearest, go even higher! and then down! and then to — the Supreme Heights! Have strength! The pain will be short, and the joy eternal. Above all, gloriously purify yourself from earthly mud! This mud was the only thing that sinned in You. Only it sins. Do not yield, be strong and have ultimate courage! Until we meet again — presently — already now —"

"Wait!" he grabbed her by the arm, even though a sublime and yet frightful chill was burning all the strength from his body. "Where are you now? In radiance or in darkness? In hell or in heaven?"

"Soon, soon you will know!" and commandingly motioning him upwards she hurried down . . . When Sider's torpid eyes glanced after her after a few moments, she could no longer be seen . . .

"Appallingly sublime . . ." his teeth chattered. "Beyond human strength . . . Suddenly I feel so weak — as if the majesty of the past few days has dropped off me like mere garments — leaving a wretched, naked worm slithering along the ground. The Divine is but alien attire, mercifully fallen from on high, oversized for the small soul. How good it is that after the grace that has trickled down to me, unworthy though I be, through your kiss, Orea, — I will promptly leave this body and this measly soul of mine before it is again engulfed by the old mud of humanity . . . 'Promptly?' Is it not — already too late? . . . I am now so very weak, so exhausted, so scorched by the fire you have set ablaze within me . . . Oh, give strength to this weakling for the final step, the final divine Leap! . . ."

Slowly he came to the summit, ruthlessly struggling with himself. "But — maybe that good little swine was right yesterday after all. Even this Errata may be nothing more than a noxious concoction of hallucinations, an unknown, diabolically fraudulent force that has inoculated my soul . . . Even Orea herself . . . Hopefully, the denouement of this farce approaches."

"Ugh, ugh! Nothing matters, save heroism! To hold You close, Orea, up there, at any cost, at the cost of death's purchase! Nothing else must cloud my mind now! Oh how ridiculous everything earthly is . . ."

He calmed down considerably and again became lucid once he was standing on the glacial plateau. The sky remained cloudless, the air still and soundless, everything glorious Death.

And there, hardly two hundred metres away — She stood — by the foot of that towering, awful cone of rock, blue like the sky. She opened her arms — and disappeared behind the surrounding boulders.

"There again, there again," he whispered to himself, white as chalk. "But I've known since time immemorial this is how it would be. So — the main battle of my life begins! To victory! Only, only victory for all eternity!"

He glanced up at the sky and with sure steps reached the ghastly cone of rock.

He started climbing up, but after just a few steps he felt his legs suddenly shaking noticeably and growing weak. "Naturally, after the tremendous exertions they've made today . . ." In a moment he realised, after a stark, dreadful quivering, rippling, buffeting of thoughts, that the cause was elsewhere : that it was a mysterious storm in the subconscious rapidly approaching over the horizon, having initially announced its arrival by manifesting itself physically. He had to sit down, and at that moment came the volcanic eruption. An awful Dread : dread of the abyss, dread of death, dread before the Ghastliness of All, dread of Orea, dread of — the *Abyss* gushed out from the depths and flooded his entire soul . . .

"This is the end . . . ; I'm not going to go through with it," he felt and groaned in the grip of the blackest despair. "I cannot. But I must. But I cannot. But I must . . . Is there anything more horrible?"

He looked up at the sky in supplication. High up above him the blue figure appeared for a brief moment before vanishing behind a rock.

"I shall go there — just up to that point, and then — we'll see," he decided and laboriously climbed higher and higher . . . It took an eternity. "I'm going to my own execution, execution by my own hand. How unfathomably shameful and dishonourable! To have to carry out a death sentence on oneself — can anything be more ignominious? What sort of unfathomable wretch must I be to allow this! What sort of wretch is a world where it is even possible to commit — suicide!" These words droned in his soul. "But," he pulled himself together, "what if it were not suicide — what if the leap were successful — what if the path has been repaired — what if the leap weren't even necessary — what if at the place where before gaped a rift the cursed Madame Cagliostro were to embrace me with laughter —"

He reached the awful cliff before the precipice, drew breath, hesitated for one more moment — then walked around it.

The rift had not disappeared, on the contrary, it had widened . . . Although leaping over it was not absolutely impossible, the chances of success versus the chances of death were 1:99 . . . Unwittingly Sider's eyes glanced down, and if he hadn't clutched the rock he would have plummeted.

He stood there for a long time, not daring to let go of the rock. And then on the other side of the chasm he saw — Her. She stood not more than twenty steps before him, her arms open. She was naked. Her body glistened brilliantly in the radiant light of the high mountains — it was shining more and more brightly, like a magnesium flame, now radiating its own light until it was ablaze like a second sun. —

Sider did not, and could not, know what was happening with him at that moment . . . Blindly and numbly he backed up several steps and started running —

But before he reached the edge of the precipice, he came to a halt and embraced the cliff.

"I cannot, I cannot, forgive me, Orea!"

"And I could —" boomed.

"I don't understand . . . Help me!"

"You must do it on your *own* now!"

"I cannot. Have mercy!"

"You have mercy! Liberate me!"

"Where are You? Are You — in damnation?"

"I am damned in all those places where you are absent."

"What am I to do?"

"Free yourself!"

"From what?"

"From yourself — Yourself! From humanity — God!"

"Oh — oh — Orea — so —"

He took a few steps towards the precipice — — he staggered and grabbed hold of the crag again. "I cannot, I cannot —"

He heard a long wail, resembling more the sharp lament of Melusine, the sudden howling of a midnight gale, than the sound of a human voice. And like an extinguished flame the solar figure disappeared. —

Half-conscious, Sider sat down on the path . . . He remained like that for a long time. Very quietly, almost inaudibly, as in a dream, the silvery sound of plangent midday bells came from Cortona . . .

"It's decided," Sider whispered finally. "I will not die. Oh, what a burden has fallen from me . . . All of a sudden I feel so light and so brave again . . . — But — what is this other burden that now weighs on me! I feel so heavy and so wretched . . . I have escaped death, more deadly than death is to be my future. — — But — perhaps not. It might only be my delusion. Away with it! . . . Beautiful nature, life, though lowly you may be, only you are certain, I embrace you!"

He stretched out his arms and felt as though all the distant rocky waves of the Alpine sea had risen up and were tumbling towards him. By escaping death there arose in him an animalistic joy of life that drove away his late low spirits and all the horrors, bringing a physical relief of equal consequence . . .

Yet, how often do all the things in this world lead to their very — opposite! . . .

"Looking at all this now," he continued his soliloquy, "it's all so comical to the point of being disgusting. The leap over this void for example — what childishness! What could possibly be its sole profound meaning? : throwing off earthliness, death, suicide. But the leap might very well have succeeded. Only a half-hearted suicide, only a half-hearted heroism. A comedy! Not a leap over to the other side of the path — a leap directly into the abyss — *that* would be uncompromising — — or rather that would have been uncompromising —"

He shuddered slightly : he felt the cowardice of this adjustment, he felt the ghastly thing he'd sloughed off knocking at his door once more . . . "Even that is comedy! Go away! To live, to live!"

"To die, to die!" he heard echoed from the closest of the horns on Stag's Head.

It was only natural that the Sublimity that had overfilled his soul the past few days could not completely vanish from it, and it was now swiftly rushing back into his soul, again refreshed and open . . .

"To die, to die . . ." he whispered to himself after a moment. "How beautiful and heroic . . . and how repulsive and trivial and low it is to live . . . Every measly insect is alive. To have the power by Divine Free Will to die at any time in glory — that is the greatest gift of the gods to humanity. To live — dishonoured before oneself — to die in madness over a period of many years . . . like Errata . . . sweet Errata — your words : The pain will be short, the joy eternal . . . do not yield, be strong and have ultimate courage . . . Ooh!"

He jumped up, his eyes burning wildly. "Am I a dog?" he cried. "How shameful it was — but it can be washed away, thank God my old strength has returned to me!"

The ringing of the bells from the depths had just faded away. Sider advanced towards the precipice. Once more he shuddered a little, and took a step back — —

"Sider! Be God!" an inhuman voice resounded from below.

He looked down. In the depths, at the bottom of the chasm, the naked figure with open arms aflame again radiated like a fragment of the sun — —

Sider's soul transformed into the final charge of a dying tiger. "How base, foul-smelling everything earthly is! What bottomless shame of shame it is to fear anything! Now is the moment to show that I am more than a mere atom of dung —"

The muscles in his legs tensed for the leap — a final brief squirming of vanquished animality — and then immediately the lightning-quick tensing of the Will commanding : *"Become!"* — whoever is capable of Will is capable of every act and all things.

And the hero threw himself into the abyss —

— — all at once — — flying through the air, it was as if his soul were swept clean of all the residue of earthly slime! There was no parade in his soul of all the events of the life now ending, as is usually the case with those plunging to their deaths — : all the radiances of imminent eternity blazed within it. He felt nothing as his ribs hit a rock ledge about fifteen metres down; falling to the ground another fifteen metres, he did not feel his legs breaking and the terrible blow to his head. Radiance prevented him from seeing how he rolled for several more metres down the steep slope into a fissure in the rock. — Then the Radiance suddenly expired. —

•

He was shown the Grace of regaining earthly consciousness once more.

He saw rock walls all around him almost at arms' reach, only to the side above him a strip of blue. He was lying in a dim, narrow hollow.

He hardly felt any pain, just as if he had been drugged. It merely seemed to him that everything, everything should indeed hurt, that in fact he did feel pain, but somewhere outside of him where He did not feel it. He looked at his arms, his legs : blood, even on the tip of his nose — blood. He felt as though amidst a steady drone he were running away from his self : "The only reason I have awoken from Death," he sensed, "is to observe it properly, and not through Its eyes, but still through earthly eyes. Thanks to You, Thanatos! The only thing interesting in life is death. Come, my companion, I will welcome You with jubilation : for I have lived well : for I am dying well, heroically."

He waited and very nearly became bored. "A pity if Divine Indifference is — boredom. No : *this* is only the child of human wretchedness. Indifference — that on high — what is it? Only Divine Radiance."

He saw something amid the rocks around him that didn't seem to be of stone. "Bones, almost decayed," he said to himself and had to labour to reach for one. "The remains of a skull — human — by all indications female. Little of it left, even though this crevice is protected from rain, snow, heat, wind, the sun. It's probably been here for quite some time . . ." He kissed it. "Why in the world did I do that? It was so natural, — I just knew . . . but it has receded into darkness. — Here is another skull, larger, certainly male . . ." He reached for it and let go immediately. "Something most strange, demented, eternally horrific has shaken me, Indifferent, what could it be? . . . Ah! . . . I know : I felt as though I were holding *my own skull* in my fingers! . . . Most horrid thought — only one dying would not be driven mad by it . . . All of it nonsense, only comic associations of ideas in the throes of agony — — What is that yellow object sparkling among the bones?" He picked up a golden, glass-fronted locket with a miniature portrait. "Oh Orea! Exactly the same as the larger one I keep here next to my heart. I can even make out the tiny letters : My Orea. — My handwriting —what was that again —it has floated off once more . . . Aaaah —"

His pathetic consciousness flew off to the place where all things are known. —

When it returned, he suddenly knew everything. It hadn't actually returned — how absurd all human expressions and thoughts are! —, but He, the mysterious Self, by a miracle that only blossoms once in a hundred years, flew into the realm of another consciousness, Another Self . . . Humankind, despite all its manifold metaphysical speculations, does not have an inkling about this, the most important thing — as is often the case : just as it does not think about death and the Sublime and Beauty and Lightness and Immanence . . . The main purpose of humanity was : fear of awakening the terrible dragon on which it sleeps, who in reality is the only Archangel of salvation.

What in Dream and Death is inherently known he now knew through the terrible connecting of what's disconnected in the waking state. And in Dream and Death it is known what existed before "birth," what existed Yesterday, but humans know only what existed yesterday, and not even that. — Sider's life of yesterday merged magically with his life of today into one whole, into a single Day of Life, and death's pitchblende iron screen between the two became transparent.

He saw himself as a young, handsome, well-to-do gentleman, who fell in love with an enchanting girl from an aristocratic family, eighteen-year-old Orea. And she fell for him with a love that burnt ten times stronger. Never did a woman love someone more intensely. Her passion was so great it completely altered her, turning a tigress into an obedient little doggy. She absconded with him from her father's house. They wandered the earth together. But his love for her soon went cold. He felt he could love her with all his heart were it not for his selfishness, all manner of passions and vices, feckless whims, the licentiousness of his polluted soul thwarting any real depth of feeling . . . He tormented Orea constantly. At first it was only from the sadism of love, later from a hatred of love, then from pure cruelty, then from pure hatred, and in the end it was just meanness and out of habit. Right up till the end she poignantly viewed all this as nothing but an expression of his love, and being, like all women for that matter, a masochist at heart, she more or less endured it with delight : the imprecations and insults, the beatings and imprisonments, the burnings and even more sophisticated forms of torture. — Finally, after three years, they took up residence in Cortona, in the cottage of Barbora, who was thirty-nine at the time, Orea's former wet nurse who loved her like a daughter. Living with them was also Orea's sister, likewise beautiful and intriguing, even though in all respects she was merely a diluted version of Orea. She fell madly, wildly in love with Sider as well, and she had run after him, and all her efforts were directed at seducing him away from her sister. And Sider did fall in love with her, too, as he did with every seductress. Together they concocted a plan to get rid of Orea — for they feared her tiger's rage if she were to realise she was no longer loved and wanted. Yet for Sider this was more than mere self-interest : it was sadism to the highest degree, a romantic desire to murder, to murder what had been dearest to him in the depths of his soul, a so-called perversity, base and spinelessly ferocious. — He knew that a boulder was poised directly above the house, and it would be possible to work it free with little effort. On one black night this is indeed what he did, so that all it would take now was to

lean firmly against the boulder — — The deed was soon con-
summated, at midnight, having earlier told Errata to spend the
night elsewhere. The roof caved in, as did the first-floor ceiling.
Running down, he found Orea unconscious in a pool of blood,
her legs injured, her face mutilated. But she was still alive, with
a deformed nose. He felt great compassion for her, his revulsion
even greater. "What fails at first must eventually succeed, come
what may!" was what he decided — and he devised a plan, as
certain to produce the desired outcome as it was safe for him, a
plan so cowardly and low, so ghastly. He knew that Orea obeyed
him unconditionally, especially since her face had been disfig-
ured, believing incessantly in his love. On 18 June he instructed
her to accompany him to the summit of Stag's Head. He also had
Errata come along so that if worse came to worse he would have
a witness to back up his story. By beating her, he managed to get
Orea all the way to the plateau of the glacier, even though she
had yet to fully recover and was hobbling — and he drove her
on to the highest of Stag Head's horns. He leapt over the place
where the path was severed — back then the gap was not as wide
— and he commanded : "Follow me!"

"Have you gone mad, my darling? Why, I can hardly stand,
let alone make such a dreadful leap —"

"On more than one occasion you've said that you would follow me wherever I go, wherever! So, now keep your promise!"

"Do you wish my death, dearest?"

"Many times you assured me that you would even go to your
death on my command! Well then, here is the place where you
can prove with action that you're not just all talk and a liar.

Well — hop! If you jump, I will love you twice as much! If you do not, it will be the last time I speak to such a craven creature as you!"

She let out a horrid yelp — Oh, how she shuddered! She would not have been able to surmount even a half-metre ditch . . . How afraid she was of death, but only because it would separate her from her beloved! . . . And yet, all of a sudden — she leapt. "Orea, don't jump!" Errata screamed at that moment and tried to grab her by the knees as she was falling, and just narrowly avoided getting pulled down into the chasm . . . Then came the appalling sound of Orea's body, once so sweet, crashing below. "I love her as much as at the beginning," Sider felt at that moment, "in fact, even more! . . . It is *I* who have fallen into the abyss, into bottomless suffering, here and in eternity, I, the most wretched of wretches! Orea, surely you're not dead, are you?" Silence, broken only by the awful, quiet weeping of Errata. "Orea — take me with you — I so want to wash away my guilt! . . ." Silence — suddenly interrupted by a maddening roar — and at the same time Sider felt a sharp blow to his back. "You despicable scum," he heard Errata's words as he was falling into the chasm . . . and the last thing he was aware of was that he had fallen into a crevice in the rock directly on top of Orea's lifeless body. Then everything was enveloped in throbbing, rumbling dreams that seemed to engulf infinity — — —

Yet there is no tale, either written or lived, that does not require continuation. — Continuation without end. — —

He knew all that now, the other dying Sider, in the same way that humans know what they were doing yesterday. But he was beginning to see much more : all previous lives, his own and those of others, and that all the lives of others are ever only His lives, His sole life, His — All; — he saw that having "killed" Orea, he had killed himself, not — his Self. And he saw Eternity, transformed — infinitely high above all human concepts — into His own Divine Self, His own Everlasting Aureole . . . And the narrow grotto, his coffin of rocks, began to burn with a flame that grew more intense and more terrible. It engulfed the pallid blue spot above him; the rotted bones flickered into flame, and the golden locket flashed up into the New Firmament, sparkling like a new fixed star — —. Between waves of multicoloured fires, as yet clouded, a flame whiter than the sun appeared, delicately, gently — the figure of a Woman! Orea Herself in celestial glory! And in the hurricane of Eternal Light he felt that his love for Her was so infinite *because* she was responsible for his horrific and beautiful fate, that his love for Her was so great because he caused Her to experience the same fate, that She loves him *so* because he brought about for both — Divine Fate . . . that the greatest Happiness was to lie here with broken bones next to the Most Beloved, whose bones he had broken . . .

He stood up — upwards he flared, transformed into Eternal Flame. And His flame and Her flame merged into a single blaze brighter than all the suns of this sickly universe. —

Another powerful, luminous wind enveloped their Uniduality — and the countenance of amorous Errata, redeemed, shimmered blissfully within it, crowned with a diadem of tears, with the aura of the Smile of Eternity, and they became a Trinity, and all the infinite lights all around streamed into It. Earthliness dissolved and vanished into Radiance, pallid Suffering melted into Delight, and everything was reborn in a superluminous, supertonal March of Eternal Victory. —

Ladislav Klíma was born on August 22, 1878, in the western Bohemian town of Domažlice. His father was a fairly well-off lawyer. At first a top student, he became steadily more rambunctious (he lost two brothers, both sisters, his mother and a grandmother during his youth), and in 1895 he was expelled from gymnasium, and all the schools in the Austrian monarchy, for insulting the ruling Habsburg dynasty. He attended school in Zagreb at his father's behest, but came home after only half a year resolved never to subject himself to formal education again. Adamantly refusing to engage in any sort of "normal" life as well, he lived alternately in the Tyrol, Železná Ruda in the Šumava Mountains, Zurich, and Prague, never seeking permanent employment, burning through any money he had inherited, and living off the occasional royalty or the sporadic largesse of his friends. He settled in Prague's Smíchov district where he wrote his first work in 1904, *The World as Consciousness and Nothing* (published anonymously and at his own expense), in which he makes the case that "the world" is just a fiction. His major inspirations were Berkeley, Schopenhauer, Nietzsche, and the Czech symbolist poet Otokar Březina. Klíma's philosophy has been called radical subjective idealism, in that all reality culminates in an absolute subject, and he developed this into the metaphysical systems of egosolism and deoessence (the subject fully understanding his substance and becoming the creator of his own divinity). These themes are also explored in his fictions, chief among which are *The Sufferings of Prince Sternenhoch* and *Glorious Nemesis*. His other major philosophical works are compilations of shorter texts : *Tractates and Dictations* (1922) and *A Second and Eternity* (1927). While only part of Klíma's oeuvre was published before his death, numerous manuscripts were edited posthumously — stories, novels, plays, and a copious correspondence (it is estimated that Klíma, in a fit of disgust, destroyed some 90% of his writings himself). And though his work was marginalised and suppressed by the Communist regime for many decades, it still managed to inspire a generation of underground artists and dissident intellectuals with its vision of one's innate ability to achieve inner freedom, to pursue spiritual sovereignty through deoessence. As the great Czech philosopher Jan Patočka aptly put it : "He was our first, untimely absurdist thinker." Klíma died of tuberculosis on April 19, 1928, and is buried in Prague.

Marek Tomin was born in Prague and grew up in England, where his family found refuge after being exiled in 1980 by the Communist regime. A graduate of Oxford University, he lives in Prague where he works as a freelance translator, journalist, documentary producer, and art curator. His translations include Pavel Z.'s *Time Is a Mid-Night Scream* and two novels by Emil Hakl : *Of Kids & Parents* (shortlisted for the Oxford-Weidenfeld Translation Prize) and *The Witch's Flight*.

Glorious Nemesis by Ladislav Klíma
is translated by Marek Tomin from the original Czech
Slavná Nemesis, first published in 1932 by Sfinx, B. Janda, Prague, in
the volume *Slavná Nemesis a jiné příběhy.* The version used for this
translation comes from the collection *Vteřiny věčnosti*,
edited by Josef Zumr (Prague : Odeon, 1967).

Cover image and title lettering by Pavel Růt
Frontispiece: *Nemesis* by Albrecht Dürer
Set in Garamond

First published in 2011 in hardcover

Twisted Spoon Press
Jeseniova 55
130 00 Prague 3
Czech Republic
www.twistedspoon.com